DIZZY WITH DESIRE

"I mean it when I say I'm here for you," Dexter said.

"Thanks," was Collette's whispered reply.

He held her gaze, and she felt a charge of electricity pass between them. Maybe it was the fact that sitting at the table with him reminded Collette of the way she'd once sat with him in this very house years ago, intimately discussing a variety of subjects, but aware of him as a man.

As if Dexter sensed the direction of her thoughts, he placed a hand on her knee. She was shocked by the brazen intimate gesture, but more shocked by the way his touch flooded her body with warmth. He stood, and then extended a hand to Collette, which she accepted.

His hands crept around her waist. "Now, there's one more thing."

Her heart pounded with anticipation. "Oh?"

He turned her in his arms. "I want to tell you how crazy you're making me."

"Dex . . ." Collette blew out a breath, hot and heavy.

"I never stopped thinking about you, Collette."

The words were like a warm ocean breeze, gently washing over her. She didn't know what to think. She felt like putty in Dexter's arms.

"In a way," he whispered, "I feel like nothing between us ever ended."

Objections formed in her mind, but she didn't voice them. His dark brown eyes had her mesmerized, daring her to defy him. And right now, she couldn't.

For he was right. It *did* feel as if things between them had never ended. Lord help her, she wanted him again. Wanted him with such ferocity it scared her.

BOOK YOUR PLACE ON OUR WEBSITE AND MAKE THE ARABESQUE ROMANCE CONNECTION!

We've created a customized website just for our very special Arabesque readers, where you can get the inside scoop on everything that's going on with Arabesque romance novels.

When you come online, you'll have the exciting opportunity to:

- View covers of upcoming books

- Learn about our future publishing schedule (listed by publication month and author)

- Find out when your favorite authors will be visiting a city near you

- Search for and order backlist books

- Check out author bios and background information

- Send e-mail to your favorite authors

- Join us in weekly chats with authors, readers and other guests

- Get writing guidelines

- AND MUCH MORE!

Visit our website at
http://www.arabesquebooks.com

HOLIDAY OF LOVE

Kayla Perrin

BET Publications, LLC
www.bet.com
www.arabesquebooks.com

ARABESQUE BOOKS are published by

BET Publications, LLC
c/o BET BOOKS
One BET Plaza
1900 W Place NE
Washington, D.C. 20018-1211

All Kensington Titles, Imprints, and Distributed Lines are available at special quantity discounts for bulk purchases for sales promotions, premiums, fund-raising, educational, or institutional use. Special book excerpts or customized printings can also be created to fit specific needs. For details, write or phone the office of the Kensington special sales manager: Kensington Publishing Corp., 850 Third Avenue, New York, NY 10022, attn: Special Sales Department, Phone: 1-800-221-2647

BET Books is a trademark of Black Entertainment Television, Inc. ARABESQUE, the ARABESQUE logo and the BET BOOKS logo are trademarks and registered trademarks.

First Printing: October, 2000
10 9 8 7 6 5 4 3 2 1

Printed in the United States of America

This book is dedicated to a wonderful writer, but even more wonderful friend, Brenda Mott.

Brenda, thanks so much for being there for me on the days I didn't think I could write another word. Your belief in me kept me going.

Continue to reach for the stars, hon. I know you'll grab one.

Prologue

Talking to him had been a waste of time. Now, as much as it hurt, she knew what she had to do.

Leaning against the solid double doors of the church, she ran her sleeve across her eyes, brushing away her tears—tears of frustration, sadness and disappointment. She wished it didn't have to be this way. She'd tried everything to get him to listen to her, to hear her out, but he wouldn't. Instead, he'd told her to leave, that this wasn't the time. Call him tomorrow, he'd said. For the past week, since the baby was born, she'd tried to talk to him, but every time he'd pushed her away. Until tonight, she'd given him the benefit of the doubt, convincing herself that he was simply too busy to talk; but now she could no longer deny the truth.

Pain gripped her heart. How could he do this to her? This wasn't the man she'd fallen in love with. That man had been sweet and caring and had always listened to her—before she'd gotten pregnant. She'd known that going to bed with him was wrong—he was married—but she'd gotten caught up in her emotions. After the first time they'd made love, he'd told her how much he cared for her, how completely happy she made him. He'd also confessed that he didn't love his wife anymore.

So she had expected him to stand by her when she became pregnant. He'd been stunned at first, like she had been, then scared. But she couldn't blame him. Given his position, people would be quick to judge. They wouldn't understand why he'd had an affair. And no doubt, they would call her a tramp. That's why she'd understood when he told her to keep a low profile. No one could know about their relationship, he'd told her, nor about her pregnancy. She believed he was working to end his marriage before the truth came out, but months later, he and his wife were still together.

Still seemingly happy to everyone at church.

While she was alone.

She no longer believed that he was going to leave his wife. Despite everything he'd said, despite all his promises, he wasn't going to take responsibility for his child. He didn't even want to see the baby. What hurt the most was the realization that he didn't want his own daughter. Yes, he was married and she knew this wouldn't be easy for him, but it certainly wasn't easy for her. For nine months, she had carried this baby, and she couldn't raise her alone. It was only fair that he give her some help.

But if he wouldn't . . .

A small whimper escaped her as she looked up at the church steeple. Behind it, the moon hung in the sky like a fluorescent balloon. A night like this should be for lovers, *she thought.*

Not for what she was about to do.

She glanced down at the baby, her precious little sleeping baby. She wished there was another way, that she had another choice. But she didn't. With her mama dead and gone, and no one else in her life, there was no way she could raise this baby alone.

She was taking a drastic measure, but if he was truly the man he said he was, he would have to do the right thing. And when he did, everything would be all right again.

Tears streamed down her face as she lowered her head to look in the baby buggy. Her daughter looked snug and warm. Peaceful. A soft smile touched her lips even as she cried. She loved this little baby so much, she'd do anything for her.

Even this.

The church social shouldn't last much longer. Someone would find her soon.

"I'm sorry, sweetheart. I have to do this. But hopefully we won't be apart for long. You'll be safe here." She stroked the baby's face, feeling her perfect, soft skin. She was a little angel—her little angel—how could she do this?

Because she had to. There was no other way. "You won't be hungry. I've left two bottles for when he finds you, okay? Your mama's doing this because she wants you to have the very best life." Her voice broke. "Because I love you so very much."

Lord help her, this was too hard. She had to leave. Get away before she changed her mind. If this was wrong, then she only hoped that God could forgive her.

She raised her head and wiped her tears. Was that a sound she heard? Nervously, she glanced around, but all she saw were the bushes rustling in the wind. Still, she couldn't help the eerie feeling that someone was out here, watching her.

She glanced down at her sleeping baby, then lowered her head to kiss her cheek. "See you soon, my angel."

A gust of wind swirled around her and she buried her neck in her jacket. She hurried down the steps and toward *the back of the church. From the open church windows came the sounds of laughter. A pang of sadness overwhelmed her. She should be inside with the other teenagers, enjoying the social. She should be like them, with her life ahead of her, not with a baby and no man and no future.*

Yes, this was the best thing. If he didn't change his mind and do right by her, at least she knew her baby would have a good home.

That thought should have comforted her, but instead she only felt as if her heart were breaking as she hustled toward the alley.

Through the open window, he watched her go. Watched her hurry along the side of the church toward the alley he knew she used to take a shortcut home.

He felt a moment of panic. Tonight's talk with her had him worried. She'd seemed desperate, agitated, and he couldn't help wondering what she would do. Would she go to his wife?

Her coming here had been brazen enough—someone could have seen them together and wondered what was wrong. Even though she'd kept a low profile during her pregnancy, he was sure some of her friends had known she'd been pregnant—friends who went to this church. How long would it take them to put two and two together if she kept coming around here to talk to him? Thankfully, he'd been able to convince her to leave before anyone had seen her tonight.

But as he watched her walk away, an uneasy feeling washed over him. Guilt, yes. He felt incredible guilt for getting involved with her. Their relationship had gone too far, and he prayed every night that God could forgive his weak-

ness. But he also felt fear. There was something about the way she'd looked at him that had frightened him.

His gut said she was going to do something drastic, something crazy that would get them both into trouble.

He glanced around the church. Everyone was preoccupied. Now was the perfect time to head out; he could disappear for a little while and no one would even notice.

Quietly, he headed toward the back of the church. One more glance around told him that no one had seen him move.

He opened the back door and escaped into the night, determined to deal with this problem once and for all.

One

Collette Jenkins sat on her living room sofa, dropping the pile of mail she'd retrieved onto her lap.

"Bill, bill, Christmas card," she said aloud as she sifted through the mail. She always checked out every piece before opening any. "Bill." Her hand paused as she came upon the next envelope. It was odd looking and definitely stood out from the rest. She lifted it for closer inspection.

The envelope was tattered, as if it had taken a beating on the way here. Collette noticed the handwriting. And felt a chill sweep over her. She studied it carefully; it was her grandmother's. But how could that be? Her grandmother had died over four months ago.

Collette's eyes darted to the postmark; August third, three days before her grandmother's death.

Today was December twentieth.

Was this some kind of joke? And if so, who could be responsible for it? As she ran her fingers over the tattered envelope and made sure the postmark wasn't forged, she realized without a doubt that this was no joke. The letter was indeed from her grandmother.

It must have been lost in the mail. That was the only possibility that made sense.

Anxious to see what the envelope held, Collette turned it over and a ran a nail under the flap. She withdrew the single sheet of paper and unfolded it.

My dear, sweet Collette.

How it hurts me to send you this letter. The last time we spoke, I'd hoped to have the courage to tell you the truth, but I didn't, and I'm sorry.

The chill Collette had felt turned colder as she wondered what on earth her grandmother meant. She and Grandma Kathryn had been so close that she couldn't imagine her keeping anything from her. So what could she be referring to?

By now, as you are reading this, I will be gone from this life. I don't want to take this burden to the grave with me. It's not right. Collette, I'm not your true grandmother. Oh, I loved you as if you were my flesh and blood, but the truth is, you're not. You were adopted.

Collette's head started to spin. She reread the last couple of sentences over and over, thinking that there had to be some mistake. Of course Grandma Kathryn was her flesh and blood. Why was she saying these things?

Knowing you, you won't want to believe it. But it's true. I only wish I had the courage to tell you

*face to face. But I didn't want to die remembering
your disappointment, only your love. Please forgive
me for telling you this way. I'm sure you'll have
questions, and if I knew the answers I'd tell you. But
I have no idea who your real parents are. I only
know that you were born in Miami. With me leaving
you, maybe it's time you find your real parents. I
don't want to think of you alone in this world.*

I will love you always.
    Sincerely,
    Grandma

Tiny prickles spread over Collette's skin. She was
so stunned she could hardly breathe.

"No," she said, jumping to her feet, refusing to
believe what she'd read. But why would her grandmother tell her this if it wasn't true?

Collette checked the exterior of the envelope. It
had been mailed from Miami, Florida, where her
grandmother had died.

Oh, God.

She sank into the softness of her plush sofa once
more, burying her face in both hands. As much as
she wanted this to all be a lie, in her heart she knew
it was true. She looked nothing like her parents, and
they were significantly older than her—her mother
forty-four when she'd been born, her father forty-six.
On more than one occasion, Collette had wondered
if she'd been adopted. She'd always dismissed the
thought as crazy—just because she was an only child
of parents whom she didn't resemble didn't make
her adopted.

Yet on some level, she'd never felt truly connected to them.

And now, she had just learned that her innermost suspicions were true. Judy and Victor Jenkins were *not* her parents.

But Grandma? Kathryn Jenkins had always felt like family. Her grandmother had practically raised her, ever since the day her parents had tragically died when the small plane returning to Miami from the Bahamas they were in crashed. That was fourteen years ago, when Collette had been only thirteen years old. Her grandmother had been seventy-seven at the time, but still strong, and she'd raised her. They'd been the only family either of them had had left, and because of that, they'd become very close. Collette hadn't wanted to leave for school in New York, but Grandma Kathryn had convinced her to go. If she was truly going to succeed as an artist, she had to go to New York, her grandmother had told her.

And she had—because her grandmother had believed in and encouraged her.

But how could she have kept something like this from her?

This being her first Christmas without her grandmother, Collette had planned to spend a quiet holiday in New York. Spencer had asked her to join him and his family for Christmas dinner, but she hadn't given him an answer. He seemed ready for a serious relationship. She wasn't. Going to Christmas dinner might be leading him on, and she didn't want to do that.

So, Collette had figured she'd work on a couple of

her paintings over the holidays. But now, she wouldn't be doing that.

Rising, she walked to the wall phone in the kitchen and lifted the receiver. She called information, then punched in the number she'd been given.

"Yes, I'm wondering how soon I can get a flight to Miami. No, one way. I'm not sure how long I'll be staying."

"I'm sorry, Spencer."

"So am I. I'd hoped to introduce you to my family."

"I know."

"Are we still on for New Year's Eve?"

"I don't think so. I'm not sure how long I'll be gone."

"Oh." He sounded disappointed.

"You know how family business can be." Her eyes scanned the framed paintings in her living room, stopping on the one picture that now held so much significance. The background of the painting was a vivid royal blue, and in the center was the figure of a black woman clutching a small black baby to her chest. The painting was so real it brought Collette to a place she hadn't been in a long time—a place where she had once felt safe. Had she ever felt her real mother's arms around her like that?

She'd painted that picture at a moment when she'd felt a void in her life, and she now realized that she hadn't painted it because she missed the mother who'd raised her, but because she missed the mother she'd never known.

How strange that in her subconscious she had known the truth all along.

"Collette?"

"Hmm? What did you say?"

"I said that if you want, I can see about getting some time off to meet you in Miami."

"No, that's okay." Spencer was a manager at a hotel in Times Square. He had a good job, and he loved her. Right now, she wished she could love him back. Maybe if she could, she wouldn't feel so empty inside. "Spencer, I know we've talked about our relationship before, but I want to say again—"

"I know. You haven't made any promises. I understand that."

He was such a sweet man. It would be so much easier if she could just return his feelings. "I guess I'm trying to tell you to . . . have a good time over the holidays. Keep your options open, okay?"

"I hear you. All right, I'll let you go. Call me from Miami if you can."

"Okay."

"And Collette, I hope that whatever you have to do works out okay."

"Thanks, Spencer."

For the past four days, Collette had been on standby at LaGuardia airport. She'd hoped to get a flight out as soon as she'd learned the truth about her life, but with it being the holidays, flights had been booked solid. There were also weather delays due to an ice storm in the Midwest, which meant she had to wait even longer. She'd almost given up when she was able to confirm a flight on Christmas day.

Christmas evening, actually. The only flight available was a red-eye, but at least it was a direct flight. She was relieved to finally be on a plane heading to Miami. Not just because she'd spent four anxious days in limbo, but because all the time she'd spent at the airport had driven home just how alone in the world she was. She'd watched as others had embraced each other, leaned on each other, been there for each other. Families. Blood relatives.

And she'd felt the hole in her heart grow larger.

If she had a real mother and father out in the world somewhere, she had to find them. Christmas was over, but God willing, she'd be with her real family for the next holiday season.

But what if they didn't want her? she wondered. What if they didn't want to be found? After all, her mother had abandoned her. Would she embrace her after all this time, or reject her again?

All her thoughts about the possibilities of what lay ahead gave her a headache, so as her flight began its ascent, she tried to get some sleep.

Three hours later, when the plane landed at Miami International Airport, she was exhausted. And by the time the taxi pulled up to the house she had once called home in southwest Miami-Dade County, as much as she wanted to immediately search the house for answers, she knew she had to get some rest.

Tomorrow, bright and early, she would start the search for her family.

Two

Dexter Harris had just placed the *mkeka*, the place-mat, on the Kwanzaa table when he heard the loud bang from next door. Looking through the living room window, he saw a light on at the back of the house.

Something's wrong. Acting on instinct, he hurried to the front door and rushed outside. If it had been any other house than the one to his immediate right, he wouldn't have been concerned. But Kathryn Jenkins had been dead for over four months and the house had been vacant since that time.

When he reached the house, Dexter tried the door and found it open. He charged inside, belatedly wondering if the intruder had a gun. Maybe he should head back to his house and call the police instead.

Too late, he realized as he saw the figure exit from a room at the back of the house. So instead he stood tall, bracing himself for a confrontation.

A loud scream permeated the air when the woman down the hallway lifted her head and saw him.

"I've already called the police. They're on their

way—" He stopped abruptly, narrowing his eyes. There was something familiar about her.

"Dexter?"

"Collette?"

For a moment, they both stood frozen, several feet separating them, their eyes locked on one another. Finally, Dexter spoke. "Collette Jenkins. I don't believe it."

"Dexter Harris." A smile broke out on her face, "You scared the life out of me!"

They both hurried toward each other, and Dexter swept her into his arms. He hugged the woman he hadn't seen in over eight years. Even after all this time, she felt good in his arms.

He broke the hug and pulled back to look at her. "Collette, what are you doing here?"

"I could ask you the same thing."

"I live next door."

"You do? I thought you were in Phoenix."

"I was." He didn't bother to ask her how she knew. No doubt her grandmother had kept her informed. Besides, he didn't care to discuss the subject of his failed marriage, which was the reason he'd left Phoenix permanently at the end of the summer. "But I'm back. I came after your grandmother's passing. I was sorry to hear about that."

"Thanks."

"I heard you were going to sell the house. Is that why you're here?"

"Sell the house?" Collette gave him a puzzled look. "Where did you hear that?"

Dexter shrugged. "My mom said she hadn't seen

you here since the funeral. I guess she just assumed . . ."

"No, I'm not planning to sell it." Frowning,
Collette stepped past him and walked toward the
front of the house. She veered right, into the living
room, and sat on one of the old sofas.

"What's wrong, Collette?"

Should she tell him that she felt like a stranger in
this house now, because all her life she'd believed a
lie? Instead of answering, she sighed.

"You miss your grandmother, don't you?"

Collette nodded. "Yeah. I do."

Dexter sat next to her, and to Collette's surprise,
her heart did a little jump in her chest. It had been
years since she'd felt anything for Dexter Harris. Why
on earth should she have a reaction to him now?

Nerves, she told herself. It had to be. Coming back
to Miami was like taking a step back in time.

"I'm sure this is hard," he told her. "Is that why
you stayed away so long? Because going through her
things was too painful?"

Collette glanced around the living room. There
were photos of her and her parents, her and her
grandmother. Why had she not realized the truth
sooner? How could she have ignored what seemed
so obvious now? She was not the Jenkins' child.

Which meant she had another mother and father,
maybe even some siblings. All her life she'd wanted
a sister or a brother and to suddenly discover she just
might have one or both was overwhelming.

"Do you have plans tonight?"

Collette turned to look at Dexter. "I want to clear out this house. Go through as much as I can."

"I understand, but why not take a break tonight and celebrate the holiday with my family?"

"The holiday is over."

"Christmas, maybe. But not Kwanzaa."

"Kwanzaa?"

"Mmm hmm. I've been celebrating it for five years now."

"I know nothing about Kwanzaa."

"That's okay. You can come and learn."

Collette stared at Dexter. Years had passed since they'd seen each other, and here they were, after all this time, sitting together like old friends. But they'd been much more than that. He'd been her first love, her first lover.

And the first and only man to break her heart.

He still looked good, tall, athletically built. Dressed in sweat pants and a T-shirt, he was as attractive as a man in a designer suit.

She'd loved him once. And she'd thought he loved her. Until he'd dumped her after securing a basketball scholarship at the University of Southern California. Her grandmother had told her that he'd gotten married shortly after his graduation. Her heart almost broke again. Then she'd moved on, determined to put him out of her life.

"I don't think that's a good idea," she told him.

He gave her a smile, one that was charming and disarming. "Come on. I don't want to think of you being here alone."

"I'll think about it."

But she had no desire to go. While she was over him, she had no interest in seeing the woman who'd stolen his heart.

Later that day, Collette stood where the gravel met the grass at the cemetery, noting the vibrant green color and immaculate condition of the lawn. Such a stark contrast to the bleak and gray atmosphere she'd left in New York City. One flight from the North to the South, and it seemed like spring had sprung over night. Birds chirped all around her, adding their happy song to what could only be described as a beautiful day.

Collette stood and took it all in. She inhaled the rich scent of the earth and looked up at the clear blue sky. She spotted two lizards on the trunk of the nearby tree. One chased the other one up the tree, disappearing in the branches.

Other than the birds and the lizards, it was only her.

Her and a thousand ghosts, she supposed.

Collette stared out at the never-ending view of headstones. Fourteen years ago on a day much like today, her parents' caskets had been lowered into this ground. And just four months ago, her grandmother had joined them.

She closed her eyes. Slowly re-opened them. Found she still felt the pain of losing them, raw and deep.

The death of her loved ones had been hard enough, but her grandmother's letter had taken even more from her—her entire past.

Collette put one foot in front of the other, then paused. She hated coming here, hated looking at gray slabs to remember those she'd loved. But she needed to be here today. She'd known that shortly after Dexter had left.

Here, she would feel closer to her family than she did at the house. And perhaps, here she would be heard.

As Collette moved forward, her feet seemed to carry her in slow motion. Over the wide expanse of graves she walked until she reached the spot beneath the sprawling branches of a cypress tree where her parents' bodies rested.

The flowers she'd planted around both sides of their headstones four months earlier, red and white impatiens, were still alive and thriving.

Life—where there was so much death.

Collette stood to the side of her mother's grave and ran a finger along the top of the granite headstone. She blew out a frazzled breath.

"Oh, Mama," she whispered. "Why didn't you tell me?"

She wiped at the lone tear that trickled down her face. "Did you think I would have loved you less? Didn't you know that I always would have loved you, no matter what?" She strolled around the back of the graves to her father's headstone. "You knew how odd I felt sometimes, Daddy. How many times did I tell you that I couldn't figure out where my interest in art came from, when neither you nor mama had been creative?" She paused. "Why didn't you tell me then, Daddy? Give me a way to understand?"

Moving to the front of the graves, she stared at the dates on the headstones, as if only standing here could give her answers.

If only . . .

Slowly, she made her way across the lawn to her grandmother's grave. A moan bubbled up in her throat. Grandma Kathryn—if there was one person she should have counted on to tell her the truth, it was her.

The flowers here were thriving as well, but Collette hardly noticed them. She sank down in the grass, onto her knees, next to the headstone.

Kathryn Elizabeth Jenkins
1909-2000.

"Grandma." Collette shook her head back and forth as she trailed her fingers over the dates of her grandmother's long life. "Grandma, why now? If you were going to tell me, why not when you were alive? Why leave me alone to deal with this, with so many unanswered questions?"

But even as those words left Collette's mouth, she knew the answer. No doubt her grandmother, like her parents, had feared how she would react to the news. But knowing that she was about to die, she didn't want to leave Collette alone in the world. Telling her now was a gift, even if she was also taking away the life she'd known.

Collette sat quietly for several minutes longer. She'd come here because she was confused, and strangely, though she hadn't received any real answers, she felt a modicum of peace. The family she'd known and loved hadn't kept the truth from her to hurt her, but to protect her. That much she knew in her heart.

"Wherever you are, Grandma, know that I love you. Mama and Daddy, I love you, too."

A gust of wind swept over her, and with it, the strangest feeling. It was almost as if the spirits of her loved ones were surrounding her.

That thought gave Collette a measure of comfort as she made her way out of the cemetery and back to the taxi that awaited her.

The sound of laughter filled the room. Everyone Dexter had invited for the first night of the Kwanzaa celebration was here: his cousins, Loretta and Rita, and Rita's husband, Blair; their five children, three boys and two girls; his mother; and a couple of his students from down the street.

Everyone but Collette.

Frowning, he glanced at the front door for the umpteenth time. She should be here by now.

"Expecting someone else, son?"

"Actually . . ." Dexter's voice trailed off as he walked toward the living room window. As he'd done this morning, he looked at the neighboring house. Lights were on in the living room and bedroom, which made him think Collette wasn't coming. "Give me a minute."

He'd go over to Collette's place. If she truly didn't want to join them for the celebration, he'd then head back alone and begin the festivities. But he hoped she would join them.

Seconds later, he knocked on her door. She answered almost immediately. "Dexter."

"Hello, Collette." He gave her a smile.

"I know I said I'd come over if I could, but right now, I just don't feel up to it. Besides," her eyes roamed over him from head to toe, "I have nothing to wear."

Dexter wore a colorful *dashiki* and a *kofia* on his head. It was a Kwanzaa custom to wear African dress, but it certainly wasn't mandatory.

"You're fine as you are," he said, his eyes taking in her casual black slacks and form-fitting white top. *More than fine,* he realized. In the years since he'd seen her, she'd rounded out in all the places a man appreciated.

He returned his eyes to her face. "I'm wearing a traditional African hat and shirt, but there isn't a dress code."

"I don't know."

"Have you eaten?"

"No."

"Then you have to come. There's more food than any of us can eat. Our eyes are bigger than our stomachs, but you know black folks."

Collette shrugged, then said, "Oh, why not?"

Dexter watched as she hustled into the nearby kitchen, grabbed a set of keys, then returned. She pulled the door shut and locked it.

He enjoyed looking at her a little too much, he realized suddenly.

"I'm ready," she announced.

Dexter turned and led the way across the lawn to his house.

When Collette entered Dexter's house, she felt as if she'd stepped into a different world. The interior looked like it belonged in Africa, which, she supposed, was the point.

She was one of three people not dressed in some type of African outfit. Another woman was casually dressed, as was a teenaged boy.

In the corner of the dining room, there was a small table, on which she saw a variety of vegetables, and a candle holder that held three red candles, three green candles, and one black one in the center. On the wall hung a green, black and red flag. In the living room was a Christmas tree, but this one was slightly different. It was decorated with ornaments of an Afrocentric rather than traditional, design.

"Collette, you remember my mother, Martha."

"Collette Jenkins?" The heavyset woman, dressed in a gold colored African gown, stepped toward Collette with her arms widespread. "Child, is that you?"

"Yes, it's me."

"Give me a hug." Martha wrapped her arms around Collette and squeezed her, gently swaying her back and forth. "It is so good to see you."

"Thanks." When Collette had come to town for her grandmother's funeral, she hadn't seen Mrs. Harris.

"I'm so sorry about your grandmother, God bless her soul. She was a good woman."

"The best," Collette acknowledged sadly. Then she looked around the room at the other guests. She wondered which of the two beautiful women across the table was Dexter's wife. The one dressed in a stunning royal blue gown struck Collette as the most likely, if for no other reason than she was also wearing an Afrocentric outfit, as was Dexter.

"Let me introduce you to everyone else," Dexter told her, as if he'd read her mind. "This is Jeremy, one of my students. And Khalid. Also one of my students."

"You're a teacher?" Collette asked.

Last she'd heard, he'd been striving for a career in the NBA. But here he was, back in Miami, working as a teacher. She wondered what had happened.

"This is my cousin, Loretta." He gestured to the pretty woman who was also casually dressed.

She was right. The beautiful woman in the stunning blue outfit with matching head wrap was his wife.

"Loretta's holding Shanika, her daughter, on her lap. That's BriAnne beside her. Jason, Omar, and Clyde."

"Wow. You have five children?"

"Oh, no." Loretta dismissed the comment with a wave of her hand. "Shanika and Omar are mine."

"Sorry," Dexter said. "I should have made that clear. Jason, Clyde and BriAnne are my other cousin's children. This is Rita." He gestured to the woman in blue. "And this is her husband, Blair."

"Hello, everyone." Collette smiled to the group. Then she leaned toward Dexter and whispered, "What about your wife? Where is she?"

"My wife?"

"Yeah." Something about the way he responded made her wonder. "You *are* married, aren't you?"

"I was."

"Oh." Oh. Not that it mattered. She and Dexter were just friends.

Dexter stood at the head of the table. *"Habari gani?"*

"Umoja," came the collective reply.

"Jeremy and Collette, I know this is your first Kwanzaa celebration. I'll try to explain things as we go along. First of all, the words I'm using come from the Swahili language. *'Habari gani'* is a greeting that means 'what's the news?' On the first night of Kwanzaa, the answer is always *'umoja.'* Umoja means unity.

"Let me start this celebration by saying how happy I am to be united with my family again this year. As some of you know, I spent the last several years in Los Angeles and Phoenix, and while I returned to Miami for the holiday season last year, it's good to finally be home. I am happy that we are together to celebrate another Kwanzaa, and that there are some new faces celebrating with us.

"As I mentioned, *umoja* means unity. It's the first principle of the *nguzo saba,* otherwise known as the seven principles of Kwanzaa. Tonight, on this first day of Kwanzaa, let us think about the importance of family, of the unity of family, and the unity of our people. If we stand up for one another, there's nothing we can't accomplish." Dexter lifted a wooden bowl. "Let us always honor our ancestors by celebrating our past."

Dexter poured a small amount of the grape juice from the bowl into a smaller bowl. "This is called a libation. I am pouring a libation in memory of our ancestors from a *kikombe cha umoja,* otherwise known as a unity cup. After this, we all take a sip from the bowl, symbolizing our unity." Dexter put the bowl to his lips and took a sip. "I praise our ancestors for their strength, their endurance, and their love. Without them, we wouldn't be here."

Dexter passed the cup to his right. Khalid accepted it, took a sip. "I praise Martin Luther King, Jr. Because of his dream, he made the world a better place for African-Americans."

Khalid passed the cup to Jeremy. "I don't know if you're supposed to praise only ancestors, but I want to praise you, Mr. Harris. Ever since you've been teaching me biology, I'm finally understanding science. You've been a great inspiration to me."

Jeremy passed the cup, and it made the rounds of the table. Each person spoke briefly about the ancestors, and some spoke of unity. After everyone was finished speaking, Dexter said, "BriAnne, will you light the first candle?"

Smiling, BriAnne accepted the lighter Dexter offered, then lit the black candle in the center of the *kinara.* She then joined Dexter's side.

"Kwanzaa is still a fairly new holiday," Dexter explained, "and families are free to create their own traditions. However, it is normal for the children to light the *mishumaa saba*, the candles, in the *kinara*. Then, the child who lights the candle for the night speaks about today's principle. BriAnne."

BriAnne smiled as she stared at everyone at the table. "Tonight, I'm going to talk about *umoja*—unity. Nelson Mandela is a man who practiced *umoja*. As a lawyer in South Africa, he tried to free blacks from the system of apartheid. However, he was put in jail because of his efforts and stayed there for twenty-seven years as a political prisoner. When he was finally released from prison, he still didn't give up the fight. Eventually, he was able to persuade the whites in power to abolish the racist system of apartheid. He later became the first black man elected as the president of South Africa in 1994.

"Nelson Mandela never wavered in his belief that all blacks should be free. He stood for what was right for his people and did what he could to bring about change. Nelson Mandela is a shining example of unity."

A round of applause went up as BriAnne finished speaking. Dexter gave her a hug before she returned to her place near her mother.

"Thank you, BriAnne, for that wonderful talk about unity. Does anyone else have anything to say on the subject?"

"When do we get to eat?" Jeremy asked, and everyone chuckled.

"Ah, I figured you might ask that question. I know

my belly has been grumbling from the delicious aroma of collard greens, cornbread, baked catfish and fried chicken. For those of you who have never celebrated Kwanzaa before, we eat the karamu, or feast, when the *nguzo saba* for the evening has been discussed by everyone who wants to contribute something. So, does anyone else want to speak about *umoja?*" No one responded.

"In that case, let's eat."

Leaning against a kitchen counter, Collette watched Dexter as he smiled and talked with everyone in the room. He seemed happy, totally in his element. Collette hadn't understood most of what he'd said, but one thing had struck a chord with her.

Unity of the family.

Somehow, as he'd spoken about unity of the family, Collette had managed to keep her emotions in check. Even afterward, when Dexter had asked how she was enjoying her first Kwanzaa experience, she'd told him she was having a good time.

But the truth was, being here had brought her more pain than pleasure. All she'd been able to think about was her sudden loss of the only family she'd known.

Shanika shrieked happily as she ran around the living room with the other children. And just like that, Collette felt her eyes mist with tears.

She dumped her plastic plate and the remainder of her food in the garbage, then hurried to the front door. She hoped to make a clean getaway and sneak out before anyone noticed her. But as she reached the door, she felt a strong hand wrap around her forearm.

"Collette."

Reluctantly, she turned.

"Collette," Dexter repeated. He gave her a concerned look. "Where are you going?"

"I . . ." She blew out a harried breath. "I just have to go."

"Already?"

"Yes."

His eyes said he was confused. "All right. Let me walk you to your door."

"No." She spoke too sharply, she realized, for shock registered on his face. "I'm sorry, Dexter. I . . . Just tell everyone I said good-bye."

Collette pulled her arm free and started out of the house.

"Wait."

But she didn't stop. Instead, she pulled the door closed, then let her hand linger on the doorknob. To Dexter, she must seem crazy, but she just couldn't stay a moment longer.

She waited on Dexter's doorstep, certain he would come after her.

When it didn't open after several seconds, she realized he wasn't going to. Which was just as well. She didn't want to tell him what was going on. But strangely, she found herself mildly disappointed.

She turned around and hurried across the lawn to the house next door, back to the house that was no longer a home; the house where strangers had raised her, not her true family.

The house she could only pray held the answers to the questions of her past.

Three

There were ghosts in this house, ghosts all around her. Ever since returning from the cemetery yesterday, she'd felt them. Yet they didn't scare her.

In a way, their presence was comforting, making her feel like she wasn't alone.

She felt them in the rush of cool air that whizzed past her as she walked down the hallway of her old home. She saw them, too; when she passed the ornate wood picture frame she'd carved years ago, she could almost see her father standing before it, admiring her handiwork. She saw them when she looked at the family photos that lined the wall of her old living room. Just standing there and staring, she could see her family members in the pictures come to life.

Collette was standing in the center of the living room, frozen to the spot as she looked at the family portraits, unable to shake the piece of the past playing out before her. Like a spectator, she could see the time she and her father had posed for a photo on a beach in north Miami. She had turned ten that day, and the family had gone to the beach to celebrate her birthday.

He chased her on the sand, finally scooping her into his arms. Collette squealed with delight. As he pressed his face against hers, they faced the camera and her mother snapped the picture.

It was one of her favorites and she was happy to see it still hung on the wall.

Yet along with the happiness came sadness, as well. Sadness because they hadn't trusted her with the truth. Many people who were adopted had parents who told them the truth from a young age. What had her parents feared? Why hadn't they told her?

Collette glanced around the living room. It was strange being here. Strange, because though years had passed, everything in the house was the same, right down to the leather recliner her father used to sit on every night while he read the paper. Strange, because she remembered everything so clearly, as if she'd taken a step back in time.

"Why are you standing here looking at pictures?" she asked herself out loud.

Because she wanted, needed, something to hold on to. A snippet of something to believe in, something that hadn't been a lie.

She wasn't being quite rational. Her time here with her parents and Grandma had been real, yet she felt like a plant that had been uprooted, like she needed a new foundation if she was going to continue to thrive.

She wanted answers, yet she had no idea where to start looking for them. Last night, after she'd returned from Dexter's, she'd searched her grandmother's room, going through the drawers and closet. She'd been hoping to find some sort of clue about her adoption but had been sidetracked when she'd found the old family albums. She'd gone through each of the eleven albums meticulously, as if looking at the pictures of the life she'd known could give her the answers she now craved.

Once again, she looked around the living room, at all the pictures that hung on the walls.

Forget the pictures. Forget the past.

She had to concentrate on the here and now if she was going to find the truth.

Before Collette got down to business, she showered, then made a breakfast of scrambled eggs and orange juice. Afterward, she felt energized and prepared to continue her search.

Her grandmother had said she was adopted, so Collette assumed that somewhere in this house there were documents that would give her more information. If she could find her natural mother's name, that would be half the battle.

Where would she find that information? Her parents' old bedroom was filled with stuff and would take forever to go through. She'd save that room for last.

She headed for her grandmother's room. She hadn't completely gone through her closet yesterday so she'd pick up where she left off.

Collette went into the bedroom and opened the closet door. There were a few shoe boxes on the floor beside all the albums she'd gone through the day before. On the closet shelf were bigger boxes. So much to go through.

She removed the three shoe boxes. Sitting cross-legged on the floor, she took one of the boxes, removed the top, and started perusing its contents. Jewelry. Tons and tons of costume jewelry.

She put that box aside and opened the next one. Inside she found a receipt. Examining it, she saw that it was for body work done on a car. The rest of the box contained other such receipts, including one for the purchase of a 1982 Dodge Reliant K car. Her parents had bought that car. Why had her grandmother kept these receipts? Because she simply hadn't thrown anything away?

If this is was an indication of what the other boxes held, it would be a while before Collette got through all of it.

Collette was replacing the lid when she heard something. A knock? Yes, she realized, hearing the knock again. There was someone at the front door.

Frowning, she contemplated ignoring it. She didn't have time for interruptions.

But there was more rapping, louder this time, so Collette rose to her feet and exited the bedroom. En route to the door she heard, "Collette, are you in there? It's Dexter."

Dexter. Collette swallowed, suddenly nervous. Why was she nervous? Of course it was him. Who else would it be?

More knocking. "Collette? Collette, are you home?"

She hurried to the door and opened it.

Dexter was already down the steps when he heard the door open. Turning, he saw her, and his full lips lifted in a smile. "Hey, Collette."

Collette's heart did a flip-flop in her chest. Why did his smile make her heart react, the way it once had in the past? Perhaps because all morning she'd been feeling nostalgic about her past in this house. That had to be why. It wasn't like she felt anything for him now.

"Hello, Dexter."

He made his way back to the door. "I didn't wake you, did I?"

"No."

Dexter gave her an odd look. "Oh. It's just that you took so long to get to the door."

"What do you want, Dexter?"

Dexter didn't like her curt tone, nor the frown that marred her lips. "I just figured I'd come by. See if you're okay."

"Why wouldn't I be okay?"

He met her eyes with serious ones. "You didn't seem okay when you left last night."

"I'm fine."

Frustrated, he folded his arms over his chest. "Then why don't you look fine?"

She merely gave a quick shake of her head.

"Can I come in?"

"If you want."

Collette took a step backward, but Dexter stayed where he was. "You see, that's exactly what I mean. 'If you want.' You sound . . . depressed or something." When she offered no explanation, he continued. "I know you, Collette. Something's wrong."

"You don't know me anymore."

For a moment, Dexter didn't know what to say. There was much between them that was unresolved, but yesterday, they'd seemed past any animosity. "Is that what this is about? Us?"

"There is no us." Turning, Collette headed toward the kitchen.

Dexter followed her, liking neither her body language nor her tone. Surely her attitude couldn't be about their past relationship.

Or could it?

Collette stood with her back to him as she leaned over the counter, her shoulders hunched forward as if the weight of the world was on her shoulders.

"Collette . . ."

"Dexter, I just want to be alone."

Dexter wasn't in the habit of ignoring women's wishes, but he couldn't do as Collette asked. He felt a strong desire to be there for her, to help ease the pain she was going through.

"If it's your grandmother's things . . ."

"It's not my grandmother." She whirled around, facing him. Her eyes were filled with sadness. "Dexter, this isn't your problem. I can deal with it."

"Deal with what?"

"God, you always were exasperating with your million and one questions." But at least she smiled as she said the words. The sad expression returned. "There's something I have to do, that's all. Something I have to figure out."

Dexter waited, expecting more. Then he realized he had no right to expect anything from her. He and Collette hadn't been a couple for years. They hadn't even kept in touch. Why should she confide in him now?

Wishful thinking. They may not be a couple anymore, but he hoped they could be friends.

"Look, Collette, I know it's been a long time since we've . . . been friends. But I want you to know that if you need someone to talk to, I'm here. I know how much it hurts to lose someone. It took me a long time to come to terms with my father's death."

"Thank you." Collette felt a twinge of guilt for being so cold. But she was confused about her life, and, to her surprise, about how she felt every time she was near Dexter. She still felt drawn to him, but maybe that was only natural; she'd once been in love with him and he was still incredibly sexy.

And that's why she was better off staying away from him, at least for now. She didn't need any mixed feelings about Dexter distracting her from finding the truth about her past.

"But right now, Dexter, I just need to be alone. Don't take it personally, okay?"

"All right." He headed for the door. "Just remember what I said. If you want to talk . . ."

"I will."

"Thanks, Mr. Harris."

"Any time, Jeremy." Dexter patted him on his shoulder as he walked beside him toward the sidewalk. Jeremy had stopped by to discuss a private matter. That matter had been his relationship with his girlfriend and the fact that all his friends were pressuring him to have sex with her. Jeremy, a genuinely good kid, wasn't ready for sex yet, and wondered if something was wrong with him. Dexter assured him that he was perfectly fine and that he shouldn't rush into anything before he was ready.

But as he watched Jeremy walk down the street, he couldn't help but shudder. Kids were having sex younger and younger these days—too young and immature for such a serious responsibility. Jeremy was only fourteen. Sadly, many of his friends had lost their virginity already.

As well as being a biology and physical education teacher, Dexter was also one of the school's counselors. He routinely spoke to high school students about their problems; peer pressure, bad grades, or grief over the loss of a loved one. He liked talking to them, and he knew they took his advice to heart. It gave him a very special feeling when a student left his classroom with a smile after entering with a frown.

Perhaps that's why he felt a little down today, because Collette hadn't let him help her with whatever problem she was facing, and when he'd left her, she was wearing a frown.

Maybe there was something more to his feelings.

"Naw." Dexter dismissed the thought before he allowed it to fully form. His relationship with Collette had been over for years, and since then he'd married—something else he didn't want to think about.

Perhaps this ambiguous emotion he was feeling

was guilt, guilt that they'd once been close yet he had allowed time and distance had come between them.

He'd forgotten to mention this evening's Kwanzaa celebration to her. Maybe he should do that now.

He glanced at the house next door and sighed. Maybe it was better to give Collette the time she wanted, because as much as he wished that things were different, he couldn't deny that too much time had passed for Collette to consider him a friend, much less a confidante.

Collette spent the better part of the day going through every single piece of paper in every single box in her grandmother's closet. She was as exhausted as if she'd run a marathon, and more frustrated than ever.

She hadn't found a thing. Not a single piece of paper that even hinted at adoption. There were two other bedrooms to be searched, hers and her late parents', but she felt discouraged. She didn't know why, but she'd figured that if there were any papers about her adoption, they would be among her grandmother's belongings. After all, her parents had been dead for fourteen years and Grandma Kathryn had been her guardian after that.

Heaving a weary sigh, Collette lay back, resting her head on the carpeted floor. Outside, darkness had fallen over Miami. That's how long she'd been in this room.

She rolled her head to the right. And that's when she caught sight of the object under the bed. Scrambling onto all fours, Collette rushed to the side of the bed and stuck her hand underneath, reaching for what she'd seen. Pulling it out, she saw that it was a medium-sized wooden box, the kind that many people used to hold special photos or letters. A memory box.

She tried to open it, but couldn't. The next instant, she realized it locked with a key. Only she didn't have the key.

Jumping to her feet, Collette hurried to the kitchen. Something told her she'd find an answer in this locked box. She dropped the box on the counter and opened the utensil drawer. Seconds later, she was grasping a sharp knife.

She used the tip of the knife to try and pry open the lock, but it didn't work. The more she tried, the more frustrated she became. All she was doing was messing up the lock so that no key would ever fit in there.

Stopping, she took a breath, tried to think. Maybe she could open the box with force. If she could just slip the knife between the crease . . .

Click. The lock broke.

A nervous laugh escaped Collette's lips.

Then, uttering a quick prayer that this was what she was looking for, she lifted the lid.

The first thing in the box was a photo of her parents. Standing closely together, they were both smiling from ear to ear. Her mother was holding a baby in her arms. Collette had never seen this picture before, but she could only assume that the baby was her.

She lifted the next item, another photo. It had been taken on the same day, but in this one, there was a man and a woman beside her parents. Collette didn't recognize them.

There were a couple more photos: Grandma Kathryn holding her, her father holding her. But beneath the photos was something else—a newspaper clipping.

Placing the pictures on the counter, Collette picked up the yellowed and tattered piece of newsprint and carefully unfolded it.

Who Is Baby Jane? the heading read.

For a moment, her heart literally stopped. When it restarted, it pounded overtime. Baby Jane? Quickly, Collette scanned the article. Key words jumped out at her. *Left on a church doorstep. Estimated to be a week old. Baby girl.*

Oh God, oh God, oh God.

Collette dropped that article and lifted another one. *Police Search For Baby Jane's Mother.* She checked the date. November fourteenth, 1973.

Her birthday was November fourth of that same year. At least that's what she'd been told.

There were more articles. More stories about Baby Jane and her missing mother. Collette was left with only one thought—an unthinkable thought.

No, she had to be wrong. There had to be a logical reason why her grandmother had kept these articles.

There was no way she could be Baby Jane.

Four

"Habari gani?" Dexter asked.

"Kujichagulia," came the collective reply.

"Kujichagulia," Dexter repeated. He looked around the table at his mother, Rita, Blair and their children. There was a smaller group at the house tonight for the Kwanzaa celebration, just family. "Otherwise known as self-determination. *Kujichagulia* is the second *nguzo saba* of Kwanzaa, and the focus the second night of this very special holiday. There were many great African-Americans who practiced *kujichagulia*, which means they followed their own path, created their own destiny. As African-Americans in this country, we know how many people have tried to control us in the past, decide for us how we should live, where we should live, what holidays we can celebrate, who we should regard as heroes. As an African-American teacher, self-determination is a value I try to instill in all my students . . ."

Dexter stopped short when he heard the pounding on his door. Urgent pounding. The kind that immediately made a person think something was wrong.

"Excuse me," he said, then made his way to the

door. He opened it and was somewhat startled when someone rushed toward him.

Collette.

"Oh, Dexter. I don't know what . . ." Collette stopped midsentence and glanced around the room. Her eyes registered shock.

"Collette, what's the matter?"

"Uh . . . nothing. I didn't realize you had company. I'm sorry." She whirled around and out the door.

"Collette!" Dexter called after her, but she was gone. Flustered, he faced his family. "Please continue the celebration without me. Jason, you were going to talk about self-determination." Pause. "Don't wait for me."

"What's going on, Dexter?" his mother asked.

"I don't know, but I intend to find out."

As Dexter closed the door behind him, he heard Jason mention the name Harriet Tubman as he began his talk, but little else.

He felt anxious with worry about Collette. She'd said that he didn't know her anymore, and maybe she was right, but he did know one thing—something serious was bothering her. And he was starting to think that it had to do with more than the fact that she'd lost her grandmother this past summer.

He knocked on her door once, twice, but she didn't answer. He was about to knock a third time when he tried the door instead. It opened. Inside, he found Collette in the kitchen, her hip resting against the counter as she stared at something in her hand.

"Collette?"

She made no response, as if she hadn't heard him. Yet he was only a few feet away from her. Slowly, he closed the distance between them, noticing the look of terror in her eyes. His stomach lurched.

"Collette, you have to tell me what's wrong."

In reply, she passed him the piece of paper she'd been holding. It was cut out from an old newspaper, and as he looked at it, he saw that it was an article from the Miami Herald.

Who Is Baby Jane?

Intrigued, Dexter quickly scanned the article, then lifted his head to face Collette.

"Someone left that baby on a church doorstep," Collette said softly. "Just threw her away."

Dexter regarded Collette curiously, unsure what to make of this article and her sad tone.

"Why would someone do that, Dexter? Why?"

He wasn't sure what she wanted him to say, because he had no idea why this article bothered her. "I don't know," he began cautiously. "But obviously the mother wanted someone to find her. Collette . . ."

"I think that's me." Her voice was a terrified whisper.

"Wait a second. What do you mean?"

"The baby. I think I'm Baby Jane."

Dexter stared at Collette for a full ten seconds before speaking. What the hell was she talking about? He'd known her parents, Victor and Judy Jenkins. How could she be Baby Jane?

"I'm not sure why you're saying this . . ."

"I received a letter from my grandmother last week."

Had she been drinking? "Your grandmother died last summer."

"The letter was lost in the mail." Moments ago, she'd sounded terrified, sad. Now, her voice sounded emotionless. "That's the only thing that makes sense."

"I don't follow you."

Collette blew out a shaky breath. "My grandmother . . . she wrote me a letter. Apparently just days before she died. She said she wasn't my real grandmother."

"What?"

"She said my parents weren't my parents. That I was adopted. And now I find this box with these articles—articles about Baby Jane." She'd been looking at the floor as she spoke, and now she met his eyes. Her face collapsed with grief. "My mother left me on a church doorstep, Dexter. What kind of mother would do that?"

Seeing Collette in so much pain, Dexter couldn't resist stepping closer to her and reaching out to stroke her face. It had been so long since he had touched her in an intimate way and he expected her to reject him, yet she turned her face into his palm.

He brought his other hand to her face, cupping that cheek. He should say something, anything, but he couldn't. Touching her made him remember the past and the way it used to be for him and Collette. He'd loved touching her, simply stroking her face, running his hands through her hair, wrapping her in a hug. She had meant everything to him then, but he'd thrown it all away.

Now wasn't the time to reminisce about the past. Not after what Collette had just told him. If it was true, it was understandable why she looked so devastated.

"Are there adoption papers?" Dexter asked, dropping his hands to his sides.

"No. At least I haven't found them." She indicated toward the wooden box on the counter. "All I found were these articles and some pictures."

"Do you mind if I check it out?"

In response, Collette stepped aside, giving Dexter full access to the box.

He went through the items meticulously, piece by piece. The gist of the articles were that a newborn baby girl had been left on the doorstep of a church in south Miami-Dade County. It had happened twenty-seven years ago. The dates of the articles spanned only a few days. Had Baby Jane's mother been found after that? If she had, why would the Jenkins have adopted her baby? The abandonment of a newborn was a big story, and Dexter could only assume that there should be a follow-up story as to what had happened to the baby.

But there was nothing like that in the box. Did that mean there *was* nothing, or that the Jenkins hadn't clipped those articles?

"Do you know these people in the pictures?" Dexter asked.

Collette shook her head. "I have no idea who they are."

Dexter took a closer look. "Well, you're wearing a christening gown, so I can only assume this was after you were adopted. Maybe this other couple was friends of your parents?"

"I've never seen them."

Dexter flipped the picture over. All that was written on the back was a date: March 3, 1974.

"Maybe they're from the congregation where your parents had you christened. Maybe even the pastor who performed the ceremony."

Collette shrugged.

"Don't give up, Collette."

"I'm sorry I disturbed you tonight." Her eyes roamed over his body from head to toe. "I thought you celebrated Kwanzaa yesterday."

"Kwanzaa lasts for seven days. There's a celebration every evening. Though in my family, we have the biggest gatherings on the first and sixth nights."

Collette hugged her torso and strolled toward the front door. "I suppose you should head back. Your family will wonder why you've been gone so long."

Dexter approached her from behind, placed his hands on her shoulders. "I'm not going anywhere."

She turned in his arms, facing him with wide, frightened eyes. "Oh, Dexter. If Judy and Victor weren't my parents, that means I have a mother and father out there somewhere. Maybe even some sisters and brothers. Aunts, uncles . . ."

Dexter wrapped his arms around her and pulled her close. "And we'll find them."

"We?"

Pulling his head back, he stared at her. "Yes. We."

A soft moan escaped her lips and she laid her head

against his shoulder. "How, Dexter? How can I find my mother when I don't know her name?"

"We'll start with the church where you were left."

"I don't know where that is."

"But I do."

Collette's head snapped up. For the first time tonight, Dexter saw a spark in her eyes. His heart filled with warmth at the realization that he'd given her hope.

"You know where the church is?"

"It's off U.S.-1 in Perrine. East of here, and not too far from the school where I teach."

When Dexter was gone, Collette lay curled on her old bed, unable to sleep. No matter what position she tried, sleep eluded her. She had too much on her mind.

While she kept wondering about her true identity and what her search would find, she found herself intermittently thinking of Dexter. When he'd stroked her face, she should have stepped away from him or pushed his hand away. Instead, she had welcomed the familiar touch.

She should feel nothing for Dexter Harris—not after the way he'd broken her heart.

For two years, she had loved him. They'd practically been inseparable during that time—the happiest she'd ever been. They'd first met in an algebra class. She'd asked the teacher a bunch of questions on the day's lesson and still didn't understand. After class, Dexter had approached her in the hallway and asked if she was still confused. When she'd told him yes, he'd offered to help her.

They'd started meeting at lunch time; Dexter chose helping her with her homework over hanging out with his friends. Then, they'd started meeting after school. Soon, they weren't discussing only algebra; they were discussing their hopes and dreams and their fears. She had dreams of becoming an artist. He had dreams of playing in the NBA. She feared not being good enough. He feared the same thing.

They had an easy rapport between them, and the thing Collette had liked most about Dexter was his ability to listen. He had been a patient instructor. She had no doubt he was fabulous in his present role of teacher.

What had started as a friendship had soon blossomed to love. When Collette's boyfriend at that time dumped her for someone else, she'd cried on Dexter's shoulder. And after she'd finished crying, they'd somehow ended up kissing.

Just like that, Collette realized she'd been denying the obvious. Sparks flew between her and Dexter. Not only was he sexy and charming, he had a great mind—and a big heart. He was always there for his friends.

She'd fallen for him—hard, and for his part, he seemed unable to get enough of her. He always held her hand when they were together and surprised her with little gifts and cards to let her know he was thinking of her. In general, he was very respectful as well as romantic, never pressuring her for sex. It wasn't until their senior year that they finally made love.

Not only had Dexter cared about her enough to wait until the time was right, he'd made sure to use a condom every time they made love.

Then, at the end of senior year, when he learned he had a basketball scholarship to the University of Southern California, he told her they were way too young for a commitment and should see other people.

Collette had been crushed. Yes, she'd been only eighteen, but she'd known then that Dexter was the man for her. And he'd always told her she was the one for him. How could he break up with her just because he was going away to school? Many couples kept up long-distance relationships.

Collette had asked him just that. He'd told her they were moving too fast, that by seeing other people, they would figure out if they were truly meant for each other. Despite the firmness in his voice, his eyes had looked sad and Collette couldn't help wondering if there was something he wasn't telling her.

He'd had a whole summer to do that, but he hadn't. Collette had been crushed. If he didn't want a commitment, fine, but she wasn't about to wait for him while he sowed his oats at college.

That's what she'd told herself as she headed to New York. Four years later, she'd learned from her grandmother that he had married.

That was when she realized how long she'd been lying to herself. She wasn't over Dexter. If she had been, the news of his marriage wouldn't have hurt her.

Now? Collette rolled onto her other side, positioning an arm under her head. Soft light from the moon illuminated the bedroom. She found herself grateful for Dexter's offer of help. As much as she wished she could do this alone, she knew that it wasn't possible. Turning to Dexter for support would be easy, just as it had been on so many occasions before.

But this time she needed to keep a clear head. As much as she appreciated his help, she couldn't allow herself to fall for him again.

Because just like before, Dexter could easily break her heart.

Five

Collette's eyes popped open as she instantly awoke. For a moment, she didn't know where she was.

Then she remembered.

It was morning. She was in Miami. In her old home.

That thought should have comforted her, but instead her stomach fluttered from fear. The house was still and quiet. Too still. Too quiet. So what had awakened her?

Collette's eyes darted around the room. She heard nothing. So why did she have the feeling that someone else was here? Not daring to move, she listened; the house was silent.

Yet she knew someone, or something was here. Like yesterday, she felt a presence in the room.

The ghost of her grandmother?

"Collette."

The voice came out of nowhere. Collette bolted upright, whipping her head to the right and left as she stared around the room. Nothing.

She wasn't going crazy. She *had* heard something.

She was wide awake so this couldn't be a dream. Who had called her name?

"Collette," came the voice again, followed by a quick knock. Collette whirled in the direction of the sound—the window.

Seeing a form through the sheer curtains covering the window, Collette jumped out of bed. She pushed the curtains aside.

Collette saw a smile spread on the face of a friend she hadn't seen in years: Felicity Hunter. Felicity pointed a finger in the direction of the front door. Collette hurried out of the bedroom to greet her.

When Collette opened the front door, Felicity said, "Girl, you sleep like the dead!" Then, stepping into the house, she threw her arms around her. "It's so good to see you!"

Collette hugged her old friend with all her strength. After a moment, she stepped back, taking hold of Felicity's hands. "How did you know I was here?"

"A little bird told me."

"Which bird?"

"I saw Dexter this morning at Winn-Dixie."

Dexter. Had he told Felicity that Collette needed a friend? Whatever the case, Collette was glad to see her. She gave her another squeeze. "I am so happy to see you. I thought you'd moved to Detroit."

"I did. But I've been back for a couple years now. It was too cold up there!"

After Collette had gone to New York, she and Felicity had kept in constant touch at first, but over the years, their correspondence had lessened until finally it had stopped. For that, Collette now felt guilty.

Felicity said, "Here we are. All back in Miami."

"I'm not back to stay."

"But at least you're here. And Dexter is here." Felicity raised an eyebrow. "That man is single, girl."

"Divorced."

"Like I said, single."

"How do you know that, anyway?"

"He told me. He always comes to the library where I work."

"Oh." Collette wondered if Dexter had ever asked Felicity about her, considering he'd known they were once good friends. She didn't ask.

Maybe he was single now, but the fact that he'd married someone else was still a hard pill to swallow. "What's new with you?"

"Nothing much. I'm working at the library. Harvey and I . . . we've been trying to have a baby for about a year now. But so far . . ." Felicity shrugged.

"I'm sorry."

"Don't be." A smile wavered on Felicity's lips. "I'm hoping it will all work out."

"Where are my manners?" Collette took Felicity's hand. "Come on. Let's sit."

Collette and Felicity sat together on the sofa. Collette gave Felicity a slow once-over. Her friend had put on several pounds over the years. Once, Felicity had been a scrawny little thing. Now, she was a full-figured woman. Collette could honestly say she'd never seen her looking better.

"How's life in the art world?" Felicity asked.

"It's going very well. I'm showing at some New York galleries, so I'm finally beginning to sell some paintings."

"That's so wonderful. I always knew you could do it."

"Thanks. It's been a struggle at times, but it's finally paying off."

"What about men?"

"You mean dating?"

"Uh huh. Men and women do that in New York too, don't they?"

"The problem in New York is everyone's so busy." Remembering Spencer, Collette released a sigh. "I've sort of been seeing someone."

"Nothing serious?"

"No."

Felicity's eyes filled with mischief, and Collette knew the direction her thoughts were moving even before she voiced them. "Maybe you and Dexter can make another love connection."

Collette's lips twisted in a wry smile. "I don't think so."

"Why not? You're both single. And you two were so in love with each other, I don't know why you ever broke up."

While Felicity had been a good friend, Collette had never had the heart to tell her the lame reason Dexter had given for breaking up. She'd been too embarrassed. "That was a long time ago."

"So?"

"So, how's your family?" Collette replied, deliberately changing the subject. "Still as dramatic as always?" Felicity was the middle child of five—and the only girl.

"Lord knows, my family is still crazy. You should have seen us all at Christmas. Don't ask me how, but we ended up in a big family quarrel. Ricky's wife isn't talking to Steven's. It's a mess. All over some foolishness. I swear, next year, I'm gonna spend Christmas in Hawaii—without them."

Felicity's family had always been boisterous, something that Collette had never understood because her family had been the exact opposite. In fact, she'd always preferred that Felicity come to her house when they spent time together.

Now, the irony was Collette wouldn't care if her family was loud and annoying—she just wanted to find them and get to know them.

"You don't know how lucky you are, Felicity."

Felicity snorted.

"No, I'm serious. You have to be thankful that you have a family."

"God, I wasn't even thinking, Collette. You miss your family. It must be harder during the holiday season."

"It's more than that. As wild as your family is, at least you know they're yours."

"Yeah," Felicity agreed slowly, giving Collette a weird look. "Collette, what exactly are you saying?"

Collette told her everything.

"Oh my God, Collette."

"I know. I still can't believe it. I know it's true, yet it doesn't seem real. And I can't stop wondering why my parents never told me. Why the *Jenkins* never told me."

"They *were* your parents, Collette. It doesn't matter that you don't share their genes. They raised you."

"I know . . ." But Collette's words trailed off. She didn't like the doubt, the questions. "You want some tea? Coffee?"

"Mint tea, if you have it."

Collette stood. "There's only regular."

"That'll do."

In the nearby kitchen she filled the kettle with water, plugged it into the wall, then opened the cupboard door. She withdrew the box of tea bags and two mugs.

How many times had she and her grandmother sat at the small kitchen table and drank tea in the mornings before she went to school? Too many to count. She didn't even have to close her eyes to see Grandma Kathryn sitting at the table right now . . . She suddenly felt like crying.

"Hey."

The sound of Felicity's voice startled her, "Huh?"

"The kettle."

"Oh." The sound of the whistling kettle suddenly registered, and Collette unplugged it from the wall.

"Hon, if there's anything I can do . . ."

"No. There's nothing. Except maybe ask some questions, find out if anyone remembers a girl who was pregnant twenty-seven years ago."

"I'll ask my parents. Maybe they'll know something."

Collette poured hot water into the two mugs on the counter. "Sugar?"

"Nope."

Collette handed Felicity a mug, then headed for the small kitchen table. Felicity followed her, taking a seat opposite her. "I'm not sure how long I'll be in town, but I'd love to have you and Harvey over for dinner sometime."

Felicity glanced down at her tea, a frown marring her features.

Collette immediately realized that something was wrong. "Hey, what is it?"

"Oh, I'm not gonna lie. Harvey and I . . . we're having problems."

"Problems?" Collette was surprised. While she hadn't kept in touch with Felicity in the last few years, she'd been a bridesmaid at her wedding and had witnessed how loving Harvey had been. Felicity had been nothing but happy with him. "What kind of problems?"

"It's all over us trying to have a baby. The stress is getting to us both, I think. We had a really big fight about it last week. I want to have tests to see what is wrong, but that costs money. He told me I was obsessed about a baby and he couldn't deal with me anymore." Felicity paused. "The next morning, he said he wanted to take me to breakfast. Silly me, I thought he had planned some nice romantic breakfast as a way to say he was sorry."

"What happened?"

"Over a Denny's Grand Slam breakfast he told me that he thinks we should separate."

"Separate?"

"Yeah," Felicity replied softly. Then she sipped her tea.

"Maybe he's just stressed out. I don't think he means it."

"He saw a lawyer on Christmas Eve."

"Oh, Felicity. I'm so sorry."

"I just can't believe this is happening to me."

"Has he talked about moving out?"

"No."

Collette shrugged. "As long as he's still there, there's hope. Maybe he's just blowing off steam. You know how men can be sometimes." With that thought, Collette's mind wandered to Dexter. He hadn't been blowing off steam when he'd told her they should see other people. This, after having a seemingly perfect relationship.

"I hope so, but I get the feeling he's serious. And maybe he's right. Maybe I am obsessed. But I want a baby so badly, Collette."

Uncomfortable, Collette swallowed. Why hadn't her mother wanted her? Why had she given her up?

"I hope you work it out," was all she could say.

"So do I," Felicity sighed. "I can't lose him, Collette. You know how long it took me to find the right man."

"I know." Felicity had gone through a few bad relationships that had left her bitter, yet she'd continued to date in hopes of finding the man of her dreams. Unlike her, Collette had pretty much given up on love after Dexter. She'd dated, but she'd never truly given her heart, afraid of getting hurt.

There was a knock on the door. Realizing it had to be Dexter, Collette jumped up. She couldn't let him see her like this, dressed only in an oversized T-shirt. She headed down the hallway.

"Aren't you going to open the door?" Felicity asked.

"You get it," Collette called. "I think it's Dexter."

"Ah," Collette heard Felicity say. She could explain that he wasn't here to rekindle a relationship, but to help her find her mother, but why bother? Knowing Felicity and how much of a romantic she was, she probably wouldn't believe her.

Quickly, Collette dressed, passed a comb through her hair, then headed back to the living room. She expected to find Felicity chatting with Dexter, but instead she found only him.

She slowed as she neared him, her heart suddenly beating wildly. Why did she still experience feelings like this when she saw him?

Maybe it was only natural. Women had such reactions to gorgeous men all the time. And Dexter was definitely a fine brother: tall, lean frame; beautiful golden brown skin; lady-killer smile. No doubt, several women had fallen for him in college.

And one had snagged his heart.

She forced that thought from her mind and spoke. "Morning, Dexter."

His eyes roamed over her lazily. Collette, self-conscious, crossed her arms over her chest. "What?"

"Nothing." He shook his head. "Nothing."

That look hadn't seemed like nothing. In fact, it

had sent a tingle of desire through her body, a feeling she had long suppressed.

A feeling best kept in check.

Yet the way Dexter was looking at her now, it was hard to stop her pulse from pounding. What was it that he couldn't say?

"Uh, are you ready?" he asked.

"Ready?"

"To go to the church."

Damn. She knew that. Why was she losing her mind around him? "Oh. Well, I haven't taken a shower yet."

"All right. What do you need? Half an hour?"

"That's fine."

"So, let's say ten o'clock. I'll meet you back here then."

Dexter drove his late-model Saturn into the parking lot of the First Baptist Church of Perrine. Tall and regal, it stood out among the other buildings on the street.

"It's so beautiful," she whispered, gazing up at the steeple.

"Yes," Dexter agreed.

At least my mother left me in a beautiful place. That thought gave her a measure of comfort.

Dexter killed the ignition and turned to her. "You ready?"

Collette drew in a deep breath. "Yes."

But while Dexter opened his door and got out of the car, Collette sat still, suddenly feeling anxious.

Twenty-seven years ago, this was where she'd been abandoned. What would she experience when she stood on the church steps? A sense of peace, or pain? Would she feel some sort of connection to her mother?

Dexter opened her door and offered her a hand. She accepted it and he led her out of the car. Her knees buckled as she stood, and Dexter caught her, wrapping a strong arm around her waist.

Her eyes met his and held. The warmest of sensations swept over her, as if she had been waiting for this moment all her life. She knew she should pull away and break the contact between them, yet being in Dexter's arms felt so right.

She saw three distinct emotions in his eyes: a hint of sadness and confusion, but desire was by far the most obvious.

Did he still have feelings for her?

"Collette." His deep voice was as smooth as velvet. His eyes never leaving hers, he brought his hand to her face and ran a finger along her lips. A shiver of longing passed over her. She could get lost in his arms, lost in the essence of him. *Good Lord, Dexter still has a piece of my heart.*

"There's something I need to say," he whispered.

Being this close to him, remembering what they once meant to each other, instantly overwhelmed Collette with sadness. She didn't want to remember the pain he had caused her. She was already dealing with one crisis in her life and dealing with residual feelings for Dexter would only be a distraction.

"No." Collette placed a finger on Dexter's lips. "Don't say anything."

"Why not, Collette? What are you afraid of?"

She pulled out of his arms. "I'm not afraid of anything."

"Aren't you?"

She met his gaze with stubborn eyes. "I'm afraid I'll never find out the truth about my mother."

Her words broke the spell of intimacy between them, which was a good thing, because it made Dexter remember why they were here—to get clues as to the identity of Collette's mother.

What had gotten into him? As he stared down at Collette, at the tender swell of her breasts under the v-neck top she wore, at her full, sweet lips, it was no mystery what had gotten into him. She was beautiful, and he was still drawn to her, as if no time had passed since they'd last been together.

He wanted to apologize for hurting her. Breaking up with her was what he most regretted in his life. He'd never forgive himself for letting his mother pressure him into doing that. "You're too young," she'd told him. "You're heading off to college—does it really make sense to commit? What's the rush?" In the end, despite Dexter's feelings for Collette, he'd been swayed by his mother's constant badgering. It wasn't that she didn't like Collette; she just didn't want him to make a mistake. And she'd given him examples of a few of his relatives who had married too young, and had later regretted it.

Maybe Dexter's will would have been stronger if he hadn't been grieving his father's sudden death during senior year. He'd had a stroke and died, and Dexter had been devastated. So while he'd loved Collette, emotionally he'd been a mess. Now, when he thought back to that time, he knew that a part of him had been afraid to keep loving her, because love brought with it pain.

Still, when he'd told Collette that they should slow things down, he'd hoped she would agree, that she would wait for him. She hadn't been able to do that. For her, it was all or nothing. He couldn't have his cake and eat it too.

They'd gone their separate ways.

Dexter knew that his youth and immaturity had played a big part in their breakup. If they'd both stayed in the same state, they might have found their way back to each other, but time and distance had come between them. Now, he wanted to explain his actions.

But this wasn't the right time—later, when this mystery was solved.

"All right," Dexter said. "Let's see what we can find out. There are a couple cars here, so someone's got to be around."

He turned and headed for the church's front doors. Collette followed him. When he reached the double doors, he tried them, but they were locked.

It was a huge church, so Dexter pounded on the door. If someone was in a back room, he wanted to make sure they heard him.

He and Collette waited. And waited.

"No one's here," Collette said, disappointment evident in her voice.

"Someone's gotta be here." Dexter pounded again, a little louder this time.

Several seconds later, the door finally opened. An older man, probably in his mid- to late-sixties, appeared.

"Can I help you?" he asked, looking at Dexter.

"Actually, yes. I'm hoping you can . . ."

Dexter stopped as the man's eyes grew wide with horror. Then, clutching his chest, he groaned and fell into a heap on the floor.

Six

"Oh my God." Collette rushed into the church and dropped to the older man's side. Tightly, he held a cross he had worn around his neck. The flat-linked chain was slackened around his collar, and Collette immediately realized that it was broken. The chain was heavy, supporting a beautiful antique silver cross with a large amethyst in its center and four smaller stones on each section around it. It took great strength to break such a strong chain so easily.

"Oh God, Dexter. Do you think he's—"

Dexter crouched on the opposite side of the man and reached for his wrist, feeling for a pulse. "He's alive," he announced. "But maybe he's had a heart attack. Damn."

The man groaned, stirred, then slowly opened his eyes. He looked up at Dexter, a confused expression on his face. After a moment, he tried to sit up.

"Careful," Dexter told him.

The man blew out a frazzled breath. "I'm okay."

"We should call someone, Dexter."

At the sound of Collette's voice, his eyes flitted to her face. As he saw her, his eyes bulged.

"What is it?" Collette asked.

He simply stared at her for a moment, almost like he was studying her. Then, "I get dizzy spells every so often. I'm all right."

"You're sure?"

"Yes," he told Collette. "Please, help me up."

He was a tall man, well-built for his age, as though he'd once played football. He looked strong, and the fact that he'd fainted unnerved Collette.

He gripped Dexter's arm. Dexter helped him to his feet. Once he was standing, he asked, "What do you want?"

"I . . . We wanted to talk to you about something." Collette paused, considered her words. "What we're going to ask might sound strange, but please hear us out. Are you by any chance the minister here?"

"Yes." He sounded wary.

"How long have you been at this church?"

"Why all the questions?"

"We'll get to that in a second," Dexter explained.

The man drew in a deep breath. "I've been here for thirty-four years."

Collette closed her eyes and whispered a quick prayer of thanks, relieved to hear what the man had said. If he had been here thirty-four years ago, that meant he'd been here when Baby Jane had been left on this church's doorstep.

When *she* had been left on the doorstep.

Hope filling her heart, she dug the article out of her purse and carefully unfolded it. She extended it to him. As he accepted it, she asked, "Do you remember this?"

The man looked at the article thoughtfully, but didn't respond.

Why wasn't he saying anything? Panic gripped Collette's heart. "Surely if you were here thirty-four years ago, you must remember."

Finally, he nodded, and Collette's shoulders sagged. *Please, God. Let him know the truth.*

"Yes, I remember this story, but I'm afraid I can't help you." He passed the article back to Collette.

"Can't help me?" Her chest rose and fell quickly as her breath came in sharp pants. "What do you mean you can't help me? The baby was left at *this* church. Your church."

Dexter placed his hands on her shoulders. "Collette . . ."

"No." She shrugged away from his touch and stepped closer to the minister. "If you know something, you have to tell me."

"Like I said, I can't help you."

Frantic, Collette whirled to face Dexter. Her eyes said *Do something*.

"Reverend . . . ?" Dexter prompted in a tone that said he was asking for the man's last name.

"Reverend Evans."

"Reverend Evans, my name is Dexter Harris, and this is Collette Jenkins. Now, I know this happened a long time ago, but if you can take a moment to think. Was there a girl you knew, maybe even a member of this congregation, who was pregnant about twenty-seven years ago? Someone who was pregnant but you never saw her with a baby?"

Reverend Evans looked at Collette. "I can't help you find your mother."

"How do you know I'm looking for my mother? How do you know *I'm* that baby?"

"It's pretty obvious," he replied matter-of-factly. "You wouldn't be here if you weren't."

"You didn't know a young woman, probably a teenager, who was pregnant around the time Baby Jane was abandoned?" Dexter asked.

The reverend shrugged. "She wasn't a member of my congregation. I'm sorry. There's nothing else I can say."

Collette turned, pressing her face to Dexter's chest. A soft moan escaped her.

"I'm sorry," the man repeated.

"It's all right," Dexter told him. He ran a hand over Collette's hair. "C'mon. Let's go."

She managed a nod, then allowed Dexter to lead her out of the church. Dexter knew she was devastated, and he felt her pain in his very soul.

Back in the parking lot, Dexter opened the door for Collette, then rounded the car to the driver's side. As he settled in he glanced at Collette.

She literally looked crushed. He would do anything to take away the sadness in her eyes, to give her hope once again. "Collette, we're gonna find your mother. I promise you that much."

"How could he not know, Dexter?" Leaning forward, she buried her face in her hands.

"This was just a start. It's far from over."

Collette didn't respond.

Reaching across the car, Dexter rested a hand on

her knee. "We still have a lot of options left, including coming back here Sunday morning. Maybe he doesn't know anything, but someone in this church might."

Collette lifted her head; there was sadness in her deep brown eyes, but there was also hope. Dexter felt his throat grow thick with emotion. He was so touched to know he could give her another reason to hang on. It wouldn't make up for the pain he'd caused her in the past, but at least he was doing what he could for her.

"Yes," she said, a smile forming on her lips. "Someone has to know something. If this is where my mother left me, she must have been from the area. Someone must have seen her, known she was pregnant."

"Exactly. We can do this, Collette. We can find your mother."

Dexter knew he'd do whatever it took to make that happen.

Dexter and Collette were quiet on the drive back. Lying back in the car seat, Collette stared at the passing cityscape as they drove, her mind lost in thought.

She was glad Dexter was here for her. He'd once been a great friend, and he was showing that time hadn't changed that fact. She needed him now, his strength, his wisdom. With Dexter around, she didn't feel so alone.

When they pulled into his driveway, Collette

turned to face him. "Thanks for going with me today. You being here for me means more than you know."

A flicker of sadness passed in Dexter's eyes. "I'm sorry I wasn't there for you before."

Collette didn't have to ask to know what he meant. He was talking about their breakup. "Dexter, that's okay."

"No. No, it's not." He paused. "Collette, I want you to know that I didn't mean to hurt you. I was young, stupid, and swayed by my mother . . ."

"It doesn't matter," she told him, though it was a lie.

"I'm sorry. I wish things could have been different for us."

Collette's heart rate doubled. She felt excitement, anxiety. But as much as she had longed to hear Dexter say this, and had dreamed of the day he would regret breaking her heart, she wasn't prepared for the myriad of emotions she felt at his confession. Maybe now, given that her whole life was upside down, it was simply too much to deal with.

And saying he was sorry wouldn't erase the fact that he'd once told her he would love her forever, then married someone else.

"Dexter, I'm not sure this is a good time."

"Life has taught me one thing, Collette. There's no time like the present. That's all we're guaranteed."

"What do you want me to say?" she whispered.

"I don't know. Maybe that you forgive me."

It wasn't too much to ask, was it? Yet granting him instant forgiveness seemed too easy.

She said, "I loved you, Dexter. I gave you all of me, and I thought you'd done the same. When you said we should cool things off, I begged you to give our relationship a chance. But you didn't. You left me, and in the process, you broke my heart. I don't know." She shook her head. "Somehow, an apology doesn't seem enough."

"I was never happy with my decision."

"But it's a decision you made," Collette replied quickly. "And you must have been happy when you married someone else."

"That was a mistake."

"Damn you, Dexter. I don't need this right now."

"Maybe not . . ."

Collette wanted to ask if he expected his words to change anything, but didn't.

"Thanks again for today." She opened the door and eased her right foot outside.

"Can you wait a minute?"

She shouldn't wait, shouldn't give him another inch, yet she paused. "Yes?"

Dexter's Adam's apple rose and fell as he swallowed. "What are you doing today?"

"I'm gonna go through more boxes. See if I can't find any record of my adoption."

"And later?"

"Why?"

"Because I'd like you to come over this evening. To join in my family's Kwanzaa festivities."

"With all due respect, Dexter, I'm trying to find my family. I have no time to sit around eating and listening to speeches."

"I know you've never celebrated Kwanzaa before. I didn't until about five years ago. But it's a special holiday. It emphasizes the strength and unity of our people, of our families. What I'm trying to say is that I think by celebrating this holiday, you might find the strength you need to face this battle. The faith to keep on going."

"I don't know, Dexter."

"This is the third day of Kwanzaa. The *nguzo saba* for the day—"

"The *what?*"

"The *nguzo saba*. The seven principles of Kwanzaa."

"Oh." Dexter might as well be speaking Chinese, that's how much sense his words made.

"Today's principle is *ujima,* which means collective work and responsibility. I can't think of a time in the last five years of my celebrating Kwanzaa when the principle of *ujima* was more appropriate. My point is that collectively, there's nothing we can't do." He paused. "Together, we can find the answers."

Collette couldn't argue with the ideal, but how often did the ideal come to pass?

"I'd love for you to join us tonight," Dexter said. "See if the celebration gives you any comfort and strength. I'm betting it will."

"I'll see if I can make it," Collette replied. "But I'm not making any promises."

* * *

Later, after spending the rest of the day going through her parents' belongings and not finding anything that resembled adoption papers, Collette had a pounding headache. She took two aspirin and retired to bed.

But she couldn't sleep. Something wasn't right. There had to be papers somewhere. She'd gone through every single piece of paper in her parents' room. If the papers weren't there and they weren't in her grandmother's room, where could they be?

Possibly right here in her own room, she thought, rolling onto her stomach. She squeezed the pillow tight. But if her parents hadn't wanted her to know about the adoption, why would they leave the papers here where she possibly could have found them? That didn't seem quite right either.

She couldn't sleep. Should she get up and look some more?

Or should she call Dexter?

The phone line was disconnected, but she did have her cell phone. Yes, she would call him. She needed to talk to him. It was only shortly after eleven, and he was probably still awake.

He answered the phone on the first ring. Collette said, "Dex, can I come over?"

Dex . . . she'd slipped so easily into using the familiar form of his name. And she hadn't planned on going to his place, she'd just wanted to hear his voice and have him reassure her that everything would be okay.

"Sure."

Collette dressed quickly in slacks and a shirt. Minutes later, she was at Dexter's door. "Hey, Dexter."

"Hey."

"Am I too late?"

"For the Kwanzaa celebration? Yeah." Dexter stood back. "Come in."

The question hadn't been sincere, of course. She just wanted to see him, to be near him, to hear his voice; but wasn't prepared to admit it to herself.

Collette strolled into the house. It was quiet but signs of recent activity were evident. The dining room table was covered with paper plates and Styrofoam cups. A roll of paper towels sat on one edge of the table. There were pots and casserole dishes that held food. The smell of the various dishes made Collette's stomach grumble.

"You hungry?" Dexter asked.

"Actually, yeah. I didn't eat dinner."

"Why not?"

"I was trying to find my adoption papers."

Dexter shook his head ruefully. "You'll be no good to yourself if you don't eat."

"I guess you're right."

"Help yourself to whatever you want."

Suddenly, Collette remembered his mother. What had she been thinking calling him so late? As far as she knew, his mother still lived here. "Where's your mother?"

"Actually, she left town this morning. Headed to New Jersey to visit her sister. She'll be there for a week."

"Oh." At least she hadn't awakened her.

Collette moved slowly to the table, her eyes taking in the décor of the house. There were paintings on the walls of African people, vistas, and animals. African carvings were on the coffee table and end tables. The small table in the corner of the dining room boasted a bowl filled with bananas, grapes, sweet potatoes, yams and tomatoes. To the side of the bowl were ears of corn. Collette noticed that the dominating colors in the room were red, black and green. A flag with each of those colors hung on the wall behind the head of the dining room table. The carved wooden candle holder lay atop a mat of red, black and green. Those were also the colors of the candles. All of these things Collette had seen two nights ago, but now she really focused on them.

Collette lifted a paper plate from the stack and helped herself to a piece of fried chicken and some potato salad.

"That's all you're going to have?"

Collette was surprised to find that Dexter was right behind her.

"It's late."

"You need to eat."

"This is fine. I'm not sure how much I can keep down, anyway."

"Because you're anxious about finding your mother?"

Collette gave a brief nod. "I don't know where to look, how to find her."

"We talked about this. We'll do everything we can. Now, sit."

Collette did. She ate the food before her, but it had no taste. Dexter sauntered to the fridge and removed a pitcher of juice. He poured her a glass, then brought it to her at the table.

"Harambee," he said. When Collette stared at him blankly, he added, "That means 'let's pull together.' "

"I feel sort of embarrassed," Collette admitted. "I'm African-American, yet I know nothing about Kwanzaa."

"You're not alone. It's a relatively new holiday, and many African-Americans don't celebrate it. But every year, more and more people discover the holiday."

"Tell me about it."

"Where do you want me to start?"

"You say it's a new holiday. How did it come about?"

Dexter pulled out the chair beside her and sat down. "Well, it's not a religious holiday, but it has a deeply rooted spiritual nature as it inspires us to live by the highest ideals and values of mankind on a daily basis.

"Kwanzaa is a holiday that honors our people and our history. Dr. Maulana Karenga, a teacher, created Kwanzaa in 1966. His vision was to remind us of our African beginnings. See the flag?" Dexter gestured to the red, black and green flag hanging on the wall. "That's called a *bendera.* "

"Yes, I've seen it before."

"Do you know what it stands for?"

"No."

"The red symbolizes the blood of our people, our struggle. The black represents the African people, and the green stands for the motherland, Africa. It also stands for our hopes and dreams for the future."

"What about that table with the fruits and candles?"

"That's the Kwanzaa table. It holds the seven symbols of Kwanzaa. As you can see, there are seven candles. There are seven principles of Kwanzaa. The holiday is celebrated over seven days. Seven is an important number for the Kwanzaa holiday."

"Wow. You know so much."

"I learned from others. Now, I'm teaching you. Hopefully, you'll one day teach someone else."

Dexter held her gaze, and Collette felt a charge of electricity pass between them. They were talking about Kwanzaa, but they may as well have been talking about the first time they'd made love—that's how much she was aware of him as a man. What was wrong with her?

Maybe it was the fact that sitting here with him reminded her of the way she'd once sat with him in this very house years ago, intimately discussing a variety of subjects.

As if Dexter sensed the direction of her thoughts, he placed a hand on her knee. Collette was shocked by the brazen intimate gesture, but more shocked by the way his touch flooded her body with warmth.

Quickly, she forced her eyes away and looked toward the Kwanzaa table; but she didn't really see the items there. Her mind was reeling with the jarring realization that she was still very much attracted to Dexter.

"Uh . . . you were going to tell me about the Kwanzaa symbols."

When Dexter didn't say anything, Collette slowly faced him. And found him still staring at her. Her breath snagged in her throat. "Why?" Her voice was a mere whisper, and she swallowed. "Why the fruits?"

Dexter removed his hand, but that did nothing to quell the fire burning within her.

"In Africa," he began, "the harvest was a time for great celebration. The harvest indicated the end of hard times. Mazao, or crops, are an important reminder of Kwanzaa's historical roots. That's why there are crops on the Kwanzaa table. The gathering of crops symbolizes the positive result of ujima, collective work and responsibility, which is one of the seven principles of Kwanzaa."

"What else is on the table?"

Dexter stood, then extended a hand to Collette. "Let me show you," Dexter said.

Collette accepted his hand, and he led her around the dining room table to the Kwanzaa table. However, once they were there, he didn't let her hand go.

"The mat on the table is called a *mkeka*. It can be any type of mat—straw, paper, cloth. Many are hand made. My mother made this one from strips of red, black and green cloth. You'll notice all the symbols are on top of the *mkeka*, which symbolizes a foundation, the fact that today has been built on the work done yesterday."

"I like that."

"Do you remember what this is?" Dexter lifted the carved wooden bowl.

"Um, I think you said it was a cup of unity or something."

He rewarded her with a smile. "Very good. It's called the *kikombe cha umoja*, otherwise known as the unity cup. When we all sip from this cup at Kwanzaa, it symbolizes our unity as a people. This cup holds the drink that we use to honor our ancestors."

Dexter replaced the cup and pointed to the corn. "The corn is known as *muhindi,* and stands for children. An ear of corn is referred to as *vibunzi.*"

"This is different from the ma—" she halted, not remembering the word.

"Mazao," Dexter finished for her.

"Mazao," Collette repeated. "Isn't the corn considered *mazao?*"

"Yes, corn is a crop, but in terms of Kwanzaa, it represents the children. There are five ears of corn here. One for each of my nieces and nephews who celebrate this holiday with me."

"Rita and Loretta's children."

"Yes."

Dexter released her hand, and Collette's stomach tingled with nerves. He hadn't simply been holding her hand as a friendly gesture, had he? And if so, why did that thought now bother her?

She got her answer when Dexter moved behind her and placed both hands on her shoulders. "See the candleholder?"

"Mmm hmm. It looks like a menorah."

"Similar, although I think the menorah has nine candles. This one is called a *kinara,* and it's the heart of the Kwanzaa table. It represents our African ancestors. Our ancestors hold us up, just as this *kinara* holds up the candles. The candles are called the *mishumaa saba.*"

"I don't know how I'll remember all this." *Especially when you're touching me like this!*

"You'll remember."

Dexter leaned his lips close to her ear as he said the words, and Collette wasn't sure if he was referring to the Kwanzaa words or to their past relationship.

As he began kneading her shoulders, she closed her eyes. Tried to fight the pleasant sensations spreading through her body.

She failed.

"You were, uh . . . saying?"

He pressed the side of his face to hers. "The *mishumaa saba* represents the seven principles of Kwanzaa. Like the *bendera,* the colors stand for the same thing. Red for the blood of our people. Black for our ancestors. Green for the motherland. The red candles are on the left, the green on the right, and a candle is lit each day of Kwanzaa for the principle we're celebrating that day."

Collette's body was so taut with emotion, she could hardly breathe. "You said today's principle was *ujima.*"

"Ah, you remembered. Collective work and responsibility." He paused. "I mean it when I say I'm here for you. I want to help you find your mother."

"Thanks," was her whispered reply.

Dexter's hands crept around her waist. "Now, there's one more thing."

Her heart pounded with anticipation. "Oh?"

"Uh huh." Holding her body against his, he turned with her so they were facing the living room. Slowly, he started walking, and Collette's body moved with him. "Some people keep the *zawadi,* or gifts, on the Kwanzaa table. The *zawadi* are rewards for the children for keeping promises throughout the year. However, this table is too small to hold all the gifts, so I keep them under the Kwanzaa tree." They were at the tree now. "Oftentimes, the *zawadi* are hand-made. But I collect little trinkets or books for the children, always something about our history.

"I won't go into all the *nguzo saba* today, but there's a list of the seven principles on the wall." Dexter pointed in the direction of where the paper hung. "You can check it out another time. Now . . ."

For a moment, Collette's heart stopped. "Now?"

He turned her in his arms. "Now, I want to tell you how crazy you're making me."

"Dex . . ."

"God, I love the way you say my name." He nuzzled his nose against hers. "I always have."

Collette blew out a breath, hot and heavy. As much as her mind said she should pull away from him, she couldn't. Didn't want to. This felt too good.

"Why are you . . . what are you doing?"

"Isn't it obvious?"

"I don't know. I'm confused."

"I never stopped thinking about you, Collette."

The words were like a warm ocean breeze, gently washing over her.

"Do you believe me?"

She did believe him. Lord knew she shouldn't, but she did. "Yes . . ."

"I don't know how I ever survived without you."

Collette didn't know what to think. While she believed him, believing him and trusting him were two different things. She'd trusted him once. After the way he'd broken her heart for no good reason, she'd be a fool to trust him again.

Which made her a fool in a big way, because right now, she felt like putty in Dexter's arms.

"In a way," he whispered, "I feel like nothing between us ever ended, that's how attracted I am to you right now."

Objections formed in Collette's mind—objections about his wife—but she didn't voice them. Right now, his dark brown eyes had her mesmerized, daring her to defy him. And right now, she couldn't.

For he was right. It *did* feel as if things between them had never ended, even though that didn't make a lick of sense.

Collette could only think of one thing—if this all ended tomorrow, she wanted to have tonight.

"Ever since I saw you again, all I've been able to think about is how beautiful you are." He nipped her neck. "Your smooth, honey-colored skin. Your breasts." Boldly, he ventured a hand to the side of her breast and softly stroked it. "Your sweet lips." Ever-so-lightly, he brushed his lips against hers. "I want you, Collette. More than seems normal."

Maybe it was the words he said, maybe it was the fact that he'd whispered them while caressing her body, or maybe it was the fact that she felt him harden against her, but her body suddenly erupted in flames. Lord help her, she wanted him again. Wanted him with such ferocity it scared her.

Finally, his lips covered hers, and it was like tasting

sweet water after dying of thirst. She threw her arms around his neck and pulled him close.

"I want to make love to you, Collette."

"Oh, Dex. I want that too."

He swept her into his arms and carried her to the bedroom.

Seven

Dexter felt as if his body would explode. His arousal strained painfully against his jeans, but he wanted to take his time, to savor Collette the way he hadn't done in years.

"God, I've missed you."

Collette purred in his arms.

Gently, he lay on top of her, covering her lips with his. She tasted sweet, like honey. He tangled his hands in her hair as he urged her closer, although they were already as close as two people could be.

No, not quite.

Dexter slipped a hand beneath her shirt and caressed her smooth, warm flesh. He'd been a fool to let her go.

His hand found her breast. Collette moaned. Her desire for him, the way every touch turned her on, raised his own longing for her to a new level. This was more than physical—the emotional connection between them was strong and tangible.

Easing himself lower, Dexter pushed Collette's shirt up. Just as he reached for the clasp of her bra, the phone rang. Hearing it, he paused, then quickly returned to the task at hand. He undid the clasp of her bra, freeing her breasts. Pale moonlight illuminated the room, allowing him to see her beautiful body.

But the phone wouldn't stop ringing.

"You should get that," Collette said.

"Damn. Who could be calling here at this time of night?" Hopping off the bed, Dexter rounded the bed to where the phone was and grabbed the receiver. "Hello?"

"Dexter, it's Cecile."

Oh, God. Not his ex-wife. Not now. He sank into the softness of the bed and spoke in a hushed tone. "This is not a good time."

"Please don't shut me out, Dexter. I'm going crazy without you."

"Well, you should have thought about that . . ." Realizing that he'd raised his voice, Dexter stopped short. "Good-bye."

"No, Dexter. Wait."

He blew a frustrated breath into the receiver. "What?"

There was a pause, and Dexter knew Cecile was thinking of something to say to keep him on the line. Finally she said, "I miss you."

"Dexter?"

That was Collette's voice, and he whirled to face her. In the darkness of the room, she met him with curious eyes.

"I'm sorry," he said. "Just a second."

"Is someone there with you?" Cecile asked.

"Good-bye," he said firmly, then hung up the

phone. Then, thinking better of that, he took the phone off the hook.

"Who was that?" Collette asked.

Dexter groaned and buried his face in his hands.

"Dexter?"

"It doesn't matter," he told her, finally turning to her again.

Collette didn't like Dexter's tone, nor the fact that he had evaded answering her question. Reality hit her like a ton of bricks. "That was your wife, wasn't it?"

"My *ex.*"

"Why's she calling you now?" Collette glanced at the digital clock. It was minutes after twelve.

"I don't know. Cecile—she's just crazy sometimes."

So the wife had a name. Of course she did, yet it hurt her to hear it. "But you married her."

"Collette, I'll be happy to tell you all about that, but this isn't the time."

"Spare me," she said, scrambling off the bed and reaching for her bra. "I don't want to know."

With lightning speed, Dexter was in front of her, reaching for her face. Collette stepped away from him.

"God, I was so stupid."

"She's my ex, Collette."

Unable to reclasp her bra, Collette drew her top over her chest in frustration. "Your ex who calls you at all hours of the night."

"My ex who sometimes gets the whacky idea that it's okay to call me from time to time. She damn well knows I want nothing to do with her." Dexter made a move toward her, but Collette stepped past him. "C'mon, Collette. Don't be like this."

At the entrance to his bedroom door, she faced him. "What was tonight about?"

"What do you mean?"

"The atmosphere. The 'I don't know how I survived without you' crap. Kissing me. Touching me." Lord, she felt like a fool. "You're still in love with your ex, aren't you?"

"No!"

She guffawed, whirling around on her heel.

Before she could escape, Dexter grabbed her by the arm and spun her back to him, drawing her body against his rock hard frame. "Don't do this, Collette. Don't walk away from me like this."

He sounded sincere, but should she trust him? He'd been sincere before but had still broken her heart. And maybe this had all happened for a reason, because she'd gotten so caught up in her feelings when she should be concentrating on finding her mother. "I have to walk away," she managed.

"Why?"

"Because this isn't why I'm here. I'm in Miami to find my mother. I don't want to get distracted. I can't *afford* to get distracted. Don't you understand?"

"No, I don't. One minute, you were ready to make love to me, now you're coming up with excuses."

She struggled against him, but he only held her more tightly in place. "Let me go, Dexter."

"Collette . . ."

Forcing her hands between their bodies, she shoved him away from her. He stood, seemingly paralyzed, the look on his face saying he was disappointed.

Well, tough. He'd disappointed her. More than disappointed her.

His wife's phone call had been just what she needed to put her head on straight again.

Groaning, Collette rolled over on the twin-sized bed, but that took her to its edge so she rolled back to the middle. Then, when she could no longer stand staring at the ceiling, she sat up.

Sunlight brightened her room. It was clearly morning and she should be up, planning a strategy to find her true mother, not moping around in bed.

She couldn't help the moping. Ever since leaving Dexter's place the night before, she berated herself for being a fool. She'd told herself to be careful around him, for she'd known he could easily snag her heart again, yet all he'd had to do was touch her and her resolve disappeared.

She still liked Dexter and hoped their friendship could blossom once again, but the last thing she needed was to get tangled in the sheets with him when she was here to find her mother.

She wasn't naïve enough to believe that Dexter wanted a relationship with her. It was all about sex. That there was still chemistry between them didn't surprise Collette. They'd always been fiercely attracted to each other.

And even if Collette deluded herself into thinking they could renew their relationship, she knew that wasn't possible. Their lives had taken two different directions—his was here in Miami, hers was in New York.

Still, as much as she'd weighed the pros and cons all night, she still felt ambiguous about the whole situation.

She didn't understand herself. It was like she had two distinct personalities; one that wanted to be only his friend, and one that wanted more than that. They constantly battled each other. Every time she placed her relationship with Dexter firmly in the past and focused on her mission, she'd realize how much she wanted him all over again.

Which, she knew, made her crazy.

What she needed to do was get up and get to work, instead of sitting here thinking about Dexter.

She showered, hoping that would sober her, but it didn't. She kept thinking about the way Dexter had kissed her, how his hands had felt around her waist.

"Stop it," she told herself as she dried her body. "You have to find your mother. That's why you're here."

The next morning, Dexter felt awful. He hadn't been able to get much sleep. All night, memories of the look of pain in Collette's eyes, of the sound of disbelief in her voice, haunted him.

Lord knew, his relationship with Cecile was over. It had been from the moment he'd learned that she'd had an affair.

He'd been attracted to her because she was beautiful, but he'd also thought she was bright and caring. But everything had changed once they'd gotten married. He'd discovered she was self-centered, and could be very mean. She didn't like his counseling kids. She didn't like him coaching basketball. She didn't want him doing anything unless it involved her.

At first, he'd thought she was simply insecure, so he'd tried to reassure her that he loved her by taking her to dinner once a week and sending her flowers, notes and cards. None of it had impressed her. In fact, when he'd surprised her at her workplace one day and found her lip-locked with another man, she'd had the nerve to blame her affair on his lack of attention.

In the end, Dexter had been happy to end their relationship. He wanted children, and she'd told him she did too, then changed her mind after they were married. It was something that was very important to him, but she wasn't willing to budge on the issue.

His glaring lapse in judgement in choosing Cecile as a life partner had left him wary of dating. In fact, he was happy with his single life.

Until he'd seen Collette again.

Maybe it was that he was already familiar with her. She wasn't like Cecile; far from it. She was not only physically beautiful, but her inner beauty shone through with every smile she gave him.

All he knew was that he wanted her. Wanted to kiss her, hold her, lie with her in bed.

And he wanted to explain to her that there was absolutely nothing going on with him and Cecile.

Dexter showered and dressed, then went next door to do exactly that.

Collette frowned when she opened the door and saw Dexter standing there, even if her heart did give a little jump of excitement.

"Dexter, I'm busy."

"I want to talk to you."

"There's nothing to talk about."

Dexter gave her a level stare. "Yes, there is. I want to tell you about my wife. Will you let me?"

"All right." Collette held up both hands in surrender, then slapped them against her thighs. "I guess I can spare a few minutes."

She led the way to the sofa, where she plopped herself down with more force than was necessary. Dexter sat in her father's old recliner across from her. She said, "Go ahead."

"First, let me tell you I am not in love with my wife."

"I thought she was your ex."

"My ex. Sorry, force of habit. Anyway, I am in no way in love with her, nor do I want to reconcile with her."

"Then why didn't you just tell me it was her on the phone when she called last night?"

Dexter shrugged. "I don't know. I guess I panicked. I was afraid of how it would look. Now, I realize that by not answering you right away, it looked like I had something to hide, but I assure you, I don't."

"Okay," Collette said softly. It was a fair enough answer.

"Cecile cheated on me. There's no going back for us."

"I'm sorry, Dex."

"It's all right. I'm over it."

Was he? Not wanting to contemplate that question, Collette stood. "Dexter, I'm glad you have an explanation, but the truth is, it really doesn't matter. All we are is friends. Whomever you choose to see is your business."

He stood and moved toward her. He was close enough for her to smell the familiar scent of his musky cologne, the same scent he'd worn years ago. "You're still mad at me?"

"I'm not mad . . ."

"Then why are you dismissing me so quickly?"

"Because there's nothing more to say."

"What about the fact that I'm still attracted to you?"

"Sexually, Dexter. You probably haven't been with anyone since your divorce—am I right?"

"Are you prying?"

"Oh, for goodness sake."

"What are you afraid of?"

"Nothing."

He took another step closer. "I don't believe you."

"Believe what you want," she said, stepping to the side. "I'm a grown woman. I certainly don't have to lie about how I'm feeling."

"No, but maybe you're not sure what you're feeling."

"I have . . . I have things to do."

Collette had meant to sound firm, but instead she'd sounded flustered. And damn Dexter; he actually had the nerve to smile at her. It irritated her.

"You think this is funny?"

"Maybe a little."

"You . . ." She placed a hand on his chest to shove him. *Man if that wasn't the wrong move!* she thought, as she felt the muscular bulge beneath his T-shirt.

Their eyes met.

She swallowed, then broke the silence. "I . . . I want you to go."

Quite easily he captured both her wrists in his hands. She didn't even put up a fight. "No you don't."

"I . . ." Her voice trailed off.

He pulled her against his rock hard chest, pinning her there as his arms encircled her waist. "I'm not the same fool I once was, Collette. You don't have to push me away."

She couldn't say a word; her head was spinning so much she wasn't sure if she'd remember the language.

"You're right. I haven't been with anyone since my divorce last year. After my wife's betrayal, I didn't think I wanted to get involved with another woman again." Pausing, Dexter pressed his lips tightly together, and Collette wondered if he was reliving the pain of his ex-wife's infidelity. "But you're different, Collette. You always were."

"Yet you married her, not me." The words stung her way down in her soul.

"I know," he said softly. "Look, we can't go back, but we can move forward. I want you to know that I meant what I said last night. About my feelings for you. How it seemed like no time had passed since we were last together."

Collette wasn't going to go there. She wasn't going to allow him to take her back to the past. She had to stay focused on the big picture. "And I meant what I said. Me being back in Miami has to be about finding my family—and only finding my family. I can't afford to get distracted."

Dexter was silent as he considered her words. "I understand." He released her and stepped backward in the small living room. Instantly, she missed his touch. "What about when you find her?"

"You mean with me and you?"

He nodded.

"I can't think that far ahead, Dex. I have to take things one day at a time."

"I still want to help you find your mother."

After what she had just told him, Collette wondered why he still wanted to assist her; because he wanted to be near her, or because he genuinely want to help? "Why, Dexter?"

"Because I know that finding your mother means everything in the world to you."

"And?"

"And . . . And maybe a part of me enjoys being around you. All right. I won't lie. A big part of me wants to be around you. But I agree, finding your mother is paramount. I won't stand in the way of your search."

Dexter was saying all the right things. Just this morning, Collette had been convinced that she should keep her distance from him, but now . . . now, she realized again how much she needed his help, his friendship. She didn't want to do this alone.

"All right," Collette said.

But she wondered if she was crazy to continue spending time with him.

Eight

"I'm not sure this will work," Collette said.

"It can't hurt," Dexter replied. "Besides, I'm sure he's hiding something. After we left the church yesterday, something kept bugging me. I don't know . . . his outright denial seems a little strange to me. I mean, this had to be a big story back then. Surely he must know something—even if it's just the name of a police officer who investigated the case. He said he wished he could help, but if that was true, why not suggest someone else we could talk to?"

Collette and Dexter were in his car, once again en route to the church. "I had a weird feeling about him, too. At first, I thought I was reading too much into it, but the way he reacted when he saw me. . . . Just before he passed out, he looked at me almost as if he'd seen a ghost."

"Hmm." Dexter scrunched his forehead in thought.

Though it was a bright, warm day, Collette felt a chill. She hugged her torso, running both hands up and down her arms. She had the feeling she was missing something, that some important clue was eluding her.

"What?" Dexter asked.

"I don't know." Collette frowned. "I just have this feeling that something's staring me in the face, but I can't see it."

At the church, there were two cars in the parking lot, just like the day before. Obviously, at least two people were here at the church. However, when Dexter knocked on the door, no one answered.

"He's got to be in there," Dexter said after a few minutes.

"He's avoiding us," Collette realized.

"There's gotta be a back door. C'mon."

Dexter started down the steps, and Collette followed him. He rounded the side of the church, heading toward the back. At the back, there was a single door. If the minister was in a back office, surely he'd hear them now.

Dexter knocked. They waited.

Nothing.

"Reverend Evans," Dexter called, knocking again. "Are you in there, Reverend?" When a few minutes passed and the reverend didn't appear, Dexter shook his head, dismayed. "He's not going to answer. I'm more convinced than ever that he has something to hide."

"You two lookin' for someone?"

Both Dexter and Collette whirled at the sound of the voice. An older black man wearing shorts and a T-shirt approached them from the opposite side of the church. Wearing a pair of gardening gloves, he held hedge clippers.

"Do you work here?" Dexter asked, echoing Collette's own thoughts.

"Yes siree. I'm the grounds keeper. I do the gardenin', pickin' up of the trash, and such. I keep the place lookin' real nice." He smiled, clearly proud of that fact.

"We were hoping to find Reverend Evans," Collette explained.

Collette saw recognition flash in the man's eyes as his gaze went to her. But how could that be? She'd never seen him before.

Yet he said, "It's you."

Collette's body stiffened. "Do I know you?"

"You was here yesterday, weren't ya?"

The small balloon of hope that this man somehow knew who she was deflated. Glumly, she nodded.

"Is the reverend here?" Dexter asked. "We've been knocking but no one's answering."

The man continued to stare at Collette. She found it both odd and unnerving.

"Sir?" Dexter prompted.

"Sorry. Sometimes I just get lost in all my thoughts, ya know? Boy, you sure do look like your mother."

Collette's heart leapt with anticipation. Oh, God. Had he just said . . . "My mother?"

"Yes siree. You sure are a dead ringer for her."

Her whole body was taut with the reality that this man could possibly hold the key to her past.

And to her future.

Collette didn't remember walking down the back

steps. She only knew she was now standing before the man, less than a foot away from him. "You know my mother?"

"Used to see her around the neighborhood."

"Who is she?" The words escaped in a frazzled breath.

"Hmm." The man frowned, placed one hand on a hip. "It was so long ago."

"Twenty-seven years," Dexter said, now at Collette's side.

"Yep," he agreed, nodding. "That's about right."

"Do you know her name?" Collette sounded high-strung, but she couldn't help it. She was so close to learning the truth.

"Can't say I do. I just remember seein' her around, ya know? Caught my eye 'cause she sure was pretty."

Collette's shoulders fell as disappointment swept over her.

"Are you sure?" Dexter asked.

Puckering his lips, the man shook his head. "I reckon it might be somethin' like Sheryl. Maybe Sherry. But I'm an old man. My brain's not what it used to be. But Reveren' Evans should be able to help y'all. He oughta know."

As the man finished his sentence, they heard the sound of a car engine. Dexter rushed from the back of the church to the church parking lot.

"Hey!" he yelled, sprinting.

"There goes the reveren' now."

Collette ran after Dexter, trying her best not to let the overwhelming feeling of desperation eat her alive. The reverend must have heard them knocking. Why hadn't he answered the door?

Why was he making a quick getaway?

Dexter chased the car all the way to the sidewalk, but the reverend didn't stop. From the sidewalk, he turned to face Collette, shrugged and flashed her a frustrated look.

He walked toward her; she walked toward him. They met halfway.

"Damn," Dexter muttered. "He knew we were here. He had to."

"He knows something." The reality terrified Collette. What could be so bad that he didn't want to talk to them?

Dexter gripped Collette's shoulders. She raised her eyes from the pavement to Dexter. "We'll come back Sunday if we have to," Dexter said. "I'll stand up right in the church and ask him what he has to hide, if that's what it takes to get him to talk."

"You don't have to wait till Sunday."

Collette turned to see the groundskeeper. She was somewhat surprised to find him standing beside them. With her disappointment over the reverend's disappearing act, she'd forgotten all about him.

"Why?" Dexter asked. "Do you know where we can reach him?"

"He'll be back here t'night. It's Friday. There's always choir practice on Fridays."

Well after dusk, Dexter and Collette returned to the church. They'd guesstimated that choir practice might begin around six or six-thirty, and now, just after seven P.M., the parking lot was filled with cars. They'd been correct.

"Wow," Dexter said, glancing around the darkened lot. "They must have a large choir. This place is almost as packed as a church on Sunday morning."

Collette didn't reply, so Dexter faced her. And found her staring down at her folded hands in her lap.

He said, "Hey."

Collette slanted her head, tendrils of her shoulder-length black hair caressing her cheek. She met his eyes. Even in the darkness of the car, Dexter could see that they were filled with sadness.

A stab of pain sliced through his heart. He'd do anything to take away her pain and confusion, anything humanly possible. He thought of the spirit of Kwanzaa and the principle of *kujichagulia*, self-determination.

"I know this is tough, Collette, but remember what I said. Don't give up. If the grounds keeper recognized you, it stands to reason that others might as well. Someone here at this church might know your mother."

"Cheryl." Collette said the name softly, pensively, as she'd done throughout the day. Every time she said it, she hoped she'd have some sort of reaction to it. Thus far, she hadn't.

Collette flinched when she felt Dexter's fingers skim her face. Her head jerked to the left, and she looked at him. His lips lifted in a faint smile as he tucked her hair behind her ear.

Just one touch ignited so many feelings within her: desire, fear, yearning, nostalgia. Why did she constantly respond to his touch? Emotionally, she was dealing with the most devastating news of her life—that she wasn't who she thought she was. Rationally, she was trying to understand why the reverend might be unwilling to talk. Both issues had her mind reeling most of the time, yet her body was still capable of experiencing sexual awareness at Dexter's touch.

Dexter's fingers lingered on her face, so Collette tilted her head to the right, moving away from his hand.

"You ready?" he asked after a moment.

"As ready as I'll ever be."

"Okay. Let's go."

Dexter cracked his door open a notch, and fear instantly gripped Collette's heart. She darted out a hand and squeezed his forearm. "Wait."

"You don't want to do this?"

"No. Yes. I don't know." She shook off the fear. "I just have a bad feeling, that's all."

"You're nervous. It's natural. That's why I'm here with you. You're not alone."

A soft smile passed over her lips. "No, I guess I'm not."

Dexter opened the door, got out, and Collette followed his lead. Within seconds, Dexter was beside her, placing an arm across her shoulder. He led her toward the church's front doors.

Even before they reached the steps, the harmonies of a lively gospel song and the sound of clapping hands filled the air. When Dexter swung open the heavy door, the decibel level increased tenfold.

Here they were, ready to get the answers she needed to solve her past.

Collette's legs felt like rubber, but she was able to put one foot in front of the other and walk through the church's foyer until she reached the double doors that led into the sanctuary. She stared through one of the glass windows, eyeing the group of people beyond. A choir of at least thirty people stood in the rostrum, while some—mostly children—sat in the church pews.

The choir sang the kind of song that lifted spirits, but it failed to lift Collette's. She was too nervous about confronting the reverend to be inspired.

Dexter pulled one of the doors open and held it. "After you."

Slowly, Collette entered the sanctuary. Being here reminded her of the countless times she and her grandmother had gone to church on Sunday mornings. But there was no joy in the memory. How could she ever go to a church again and not remember that she'd been abandoned by her mother?

Collette glanced around. With all the people here, she couldn't help thinking of Dexter's words—if not the reverend, then maybe a member of his congregation might be able to help her. She'd been left at this church, which meant her mother had lived in the area. There was always a chance her mother had traveled from a faraway neighborhood so she could leave her baby at a church where no one knew her, but Collette doubted that. Besides, if the groundskeeper had all his faculties—and she had no reason to think that he didn't—then her mother had definitely lived nearby.

Her eyes roamed the church. The wisp of a memory flashed in and out of Collette's mind, too quick to grasp. What was it that bothered her?

The feel of Dexter's hands on her shoulders jolted her from her thoughts. "People are staring," he said. "Let's sit."

Dexter turned her body slightly to the left, directing her to the back pew. They both sat.

Collette continued glancing around. "I don't see the reverend."

"There he is, in the rostrum, behind the choir. He's sitting in the pew to the right."

Collette spotted him. Clearly, he had spotted her, too, for he was staring at her from across the room. She didn't look away, silently letting him know she was here. After a moment, he broke their eye contact.

"He's seen us," Collette said. "What should we do, Dexter? Wait until the practice is over before we try to talk to him?"

"Whatever he knows, we want him to cooperate, not get angry with us, which is exactly what could happen if we try to approach him now. Yeah, we should wait."

"I don't know how long I can sit here." Collette pressed a hand to her belly. "My stomach is so antsy."

The song ended, and curious choir members stared in their direction. That didn't bother her. They were new faces in the church; people were bound to wonder why they were here. But the reverend was suddenly ignoring them.

The choir master led the group in another song, then another, before she thanked everyone for coming and reminded them to be at the church bright and early Sunday morning.

The members finally began to disburse.

The men and women made their way down the aisle toward the back pews where Dexter and Collette sat. Thus far, the minister still sat in the rostrum. Standing, Dexter watched him. He'd spotted them, but as he lingered, he deliberately avoided looking in their direction. The good reverend didn't want to see them.

"May I help you?"

Surprised at the voice, Dexter turned and faced the man who'd spoken. Approximately six feet tall, the attractive looking man looked to be in his late thirties, early forties. "No, thanks." Dexter gave the man a polite nod. "We're waiting for someone."

The man's eyes went back and forth between Collette, who still sat, and Dexter, who was standing. "You're sure? Because if there's something I can help you with . . ."

"No," Dexter assured him in a tone that left no room for further discussion.

But the man didn't back down. He crossed his thick arms over his chest. "You're not here to see Reverend Evans by any chance, are you?"

The man's question was dead-on, and in no way a coincidence. Had the reverend sent this guy to get rid of them?

Dexter threw a quick glance in the direction of the

altar. The reverend was gone! But a second later, he spotted the older man in front of the pulpit.

"Excuse me," Dexter said, stepping toward the aisle.

The man flashed him a sardonic smile as he blocked his path. "I believe my father has said all he has to say to you."

Dexter's eyes narrowed on the man. "You're Reverend Evans's son?"

"Jabari Evans. Now, while we welcome anyone who wants to worship with us, we do reserve the right to ask people to leave if we think they're here to cause trouble."

"Is that so?" Dexter's tone was mocking. "And what would give you the idea that we're here to cause trouble?"

"All I know is that my father said he's already answered your questions. I'm not sure why you've returned."

"Funny, I don't remember him answering anything."

Jabari leveled cold eyes on Dexter. "Look, my father doesn't want to talk to you. So, if you don't mind."

"He's leaving!" Collette exclaimed.

Dexter pushed his way into the aisle, but Jabari grabbed his arm. Dexter's eyes fell to the man's offending hand. "Take your hand off me."

As Dexter had been dealing with the reverend's son, Collette remained quiet. She'd been keeping her eyes on the reverend, making sure he didn't make a hasty getaway like he'd done earlier today.

But now, realizing that the tension between Dexter and Jabari was quickly escalating, she shot to her feet and positioned herself between them. The last thing they needed was a fight in the church. "We're not here to cause any trouble, Jabari. I assure you that."

Dexter jerked his arm free. "Collette, go out the front. I'll see if I can catch him at the back."

Dexter took off down the aisle. Heads whirled in his direction as people no doubt wondered what was going on. Collette watched him for only a second before she pivoted on her heel to head in the opposite direction.

Jabari grabbed her forearm before she could escape. "Not so fast."

Collette tried to wring her arm free, but Jabari wouldn't let her go. Meeting his eyes, she saw that he looked at her with what could only be described as contempt. Why? What had his father told him?

"We're leaving. That's what you want, isn't it?"

"I'm not going to let you harass my father."

Again, Collette tried to free her arm, but Jabari tightened his grip. "What's your father afraid of?"

"He doesn't like troublemakers. Neither do I."

"You're hurting me."

Glaring at her, Jabari dropped her arm. Collette didn't waste a second before turning and fleeing from the church.

Outside, she stared into the darkness for a sign of Dexter or the reverend. She heard the sound of squealing tires as a car peeled out of the church lot.

The reverend. He'd gotten away again!

Collette flew down the church steps, running toward the center of the parking lot. There were many people there, but she didn't see Dexter. Whirling around, she looked for him among the crowd. Where was he?

Two arms grabbed her from behind. She screamed.

"It's me, Collette. Dexter."

Relieved, Collette spun around, facing him. "Did you get to talk to him?"

"No."

"Damn. I tried to leave the church when you did, but Jabari stopped me. I swear, I've never met such a jerk in a house of worship. He dug his nails into my arm."

"That son of a . . ." Dexter started toward the church.

Collette darted after him, scurrying in front of him to block his path. "No, Dex. Don't."

"He had no right to lay a hand on you."

"Let's just forget it," Collette said. "The guy gives me the creeps."

Dexter ground out a frustrated grunt, then, his shoulders drooping, he draped an arm around Collette. "I'm sorry, sweetie. I'd hoped to get some answers for you."

"It's okay. We'll come back on Sunday." While before Collette had been anxious about facing the minister again, now she was angry, and more determined than ever to get at the truth.

The sound of the church's front door opening made Collette look in that direction. Two women, one who looked to be in her late fifties, the other significantly older, stepped outside, followed by Jabari. The women headed down the steps while Jabari stayed to lock the door.

Collette felt Dexter's body tense. She placed a hand on his chest. "Dex, don't."

"I won't. But I want him to know he hasn't intimidated us."

Collette's eyes were glued on Jabari. She watched him turn and shoot an angry look in their direction. Despite being at a church, and despite him being the son of a minister, the man seemed ready for a confrontation.

Hardly a natural reaction to strangers who just wanted to ask a few questions.

As Jabari slowly made his way down the steps, Collette could feel Dexter's heart rate accelerating beneath her palm. This was crazy. They needed to get out of here. Jabari wasn't going to give them any answers, so there was no point pressing the issue further and possibly getting into an ugly dispute.

She was gently urging Dexter to move when she heard, "You! You stay away from here. You're the devil's child! Pure evil!"

At the sound of the hissing voice, Collette's head snapped around so fast, she heard her neck crack. She found herself staring into the bulging, wild eyes of the old lady who'd exited the church moments ago. The woman thrust her Bible forward with both hands, as if trying to ward off demons.

As if *Collette* were a demon.

A tingle raced down Collette's spine. Something made her ask, "Do you know me?"

The old woman didn't answer, just held her Bible firmly before her as she took slow, deliberate steps backward.

Dumbfounded, Collette could only stare.

When she'd put a significant distance between them, the old lady turned and hurried to the car where Jabari and the other woman stood.

Collette couldn't help feeling she'd just come face-to-face with the devil.

Nine

"Uh-oh." Seeing the group of people on his doorstep, Dexter immediately realized the time—and his major faux pas. It was the fourth night of Kwanzaa and his guests were here for the celebration. Rita sat on the top step beside a woman he'd never seen before, while BriAnne, Jason and Clyde romped around the yard. Blair leaned against the front door.

"Oh, Dex. I'm sorry. You were supposed to celebrate Kwanzaa with your family tonight, weren't you?"

"Yeah. And I forgot that my mother's out of town. Damn. There was no one here to open the door."

It was a comfortably warm Miami evening, with just the hint of a breeze that rustled the leaves of the sprawling Banyan tree on his front lawn. At least his family wouldn't freeze to death in these conditions.

By the time Dexter had the car parked and he and Collette were getting out, Rita was walking toward them. "Well, well, well," she chastised playfully. "Look who finally showed up."

"I'm sorry."

"You should be." But Rita had a smile in her voice.

She wrapped her arms around Dexter and squeezed him. *"Kwanzaa yenu iwe na hen!"*

"That means 'Happy Kwanzaa'," Dexter explained to Collette as he and his cousin pulled apart.

"Hello, Collette."

"Hello, Rita. I must apologize. I'm the reason Dexter is late."

"Mmm hmm." Rita looked at them both like they'd been caught making out in the back seat of the car.

Too late, Collette realized how her words had sounded. She opened her mouth to clarify, but Rita spoke before she did.

"Come meet Nadine." Rita linked arms with Dexter and led him toward the house.

Collette stood back a moment, watching the children excitedly gather around Dexter. He ran a hand over BriAnne's hair, then stooped to pick up the two boys at the same time. Collette estimated them to be about six and seven, while BriAnne looked to be about twelve.

Instead of experiencing the familiar longing for her own family, she felt a moment of happiness. Dexter was truly wonderful with children; patient, willing to listen, fun. It was no wonder he'd gone into teaching.

For the first time, she realized that she hadn't asked Dexter what had happened to his dream of a career in the NBA. Since she'd returned to Miami, she'd been obsessed with her own life's mystery.

"Is this the first time you've celebrated Kwanzaa?"

Dexter was asking Nadine when Collette strolled up to them.

"Yes. Rita has been pestering me since last week to join you."

"Nadine works at the nail salon across the street from me," Rita explained, flashing her long, acrylic nails.

"Well, I'm glad you decided to join us. *Harambee!*"

Everyone gathered around Dexter as he opened the front door, then followed him into the house. Dexter flicked the light switch on the wall, illuminating the room.

"Can I light the candles now?" BriAnne danced with excitement at Dexter's feet.

Dexter palmed her face. "The lighter's on the table. Go ahead."

BriAnne ran off in the direction of the Kwanzaa table, followed by her two brothers. Curious, Collette lagged behind them. She watched as BriAnne lit the black candle in the center of the *kinara,* then the red candle on the immediate left, followed by the green candle at the immediate right. Lastly, she lit another red candle next to the one that was already burning. The glow of the candles danced across BriAnne's face, brightening her wide-with-excitement light brown eyes.

Four candles, Collette realized. This was the fourth day of Kwanzaa. A candle was lit each day.

"I still have food from yesterday," Dexter announced. "Sandwiches, fried chicken, sweet potato pie. But of course, that comes later." He opened the fridge and withdrew a pitcher. "Collette, can you bring me the *kikombe cha umoja?*"

"Oh . . . sure." Collette glanced at the items on the Kwanzaa table, trying to remember what was what. Given the fact that he held a juice pitcher, he had to be referring to the wooden bowl. The unity cup. Her lips curling in a smile, Collette reached for the bowl.

"Very good." Dexter winked at her when she handed him the bowl. "You're remembering."

"I guess I am."

Dexter turned on the sink faucets and ran the bowl under the water. "I normally have the unity cup filled with libation before everyone arrives, ready to pour the *tambiko* in honor of our ancestors."

"I'm sorry, Dexter. This is my fault."

"Hey," he said matter-of-factly. "I told you I'm gonna be there for you. Besides, it doesn't look like anyone's bothered by the slight delay."

Collette surveyed the living room, where everyone was talking and laughing. No harm done.

"Harambee." Dexter carried the unity cup to the dining room table. Heeding his call, everyone made their way to the table and joined him. Dexter took his place at the head of the table. *"Habari gani?"*

"Ujamaa!" BriAnne's, Jason's and Clyde's voices carried loudly above the rest.

"Ujamaa," Dexter repeated. "Cooperative economics. This is the fourth principle of Kwanzaa, and it invokes us to open, maintain, and support black businesses. Oftentimes when we go shopping, we go to stores that aren't owned by blacks. Why is that?

Shouldn't we support our own people's business endeavors?" There were nods of agreement. "Why not go to black doctors? Black mechanics? Black-owned grocery stores and restaurants? When we support our people economically, it helps us create a stronger community."

"Amen," Rita chimed.

"I honor our ancestors who practiced *ujamaa.*" Dexter lifted the *kikombe cha umoja* and poured some grape juice into a smaller wooden bowl. "I honor Biddy Mason, who was once a slave and went on to make a good living as a free woman in California. I honor her because she gave back to her community by donating money to build schools, churches and nursing homes for our people."

Dexter took a sip from the *kikombe cha umoja,* then passed it to his right.

Collette watched and listened with fascination as each person at the table honored their ancestors. So far, everything she was learning about Kwanzaa was wonderful. All the principles she'd learned were not only inspiring, they made her think of herself as an African-American and what role she played in her own community. As much as possible she tried to support other blacks, especially other black artists. If she was in a bookstore and a black author was doing a signing, she made sure to buy a book.

She'd been practicing *ujamaa,* but until today hadn't known it. No doubt there was more she could do, and Kwanzaa was making her think about those things. Indeed it was a special holiday, celebrating the good of African-Americans and their communities.

Nadine passed the cup to her. Accepting it, Collette thought about someone in history who had practiced *ujamaa*. "I honor A. Philip Randolph," she announced. "I know that he organized the first black trade union for those who worked on the railroads, which resulted in better job conditions and higher wages." She shrugged and giggled nervously, not knowing what else to say. "I . . . I honor him." She lifted the unity cup to her lips and sipped some of the grape juice.

As she passed the cup to Dexter, she felt a surge of pride. Pride at being African-American and having a history rich in wonderful traditions. Pride at taking part in this ceremony instead of being an observer.

Dexter asked, "Does anyone care to comment on *ujamaa*?"

Rita nudged Clyde. "Go on, honey. What did we discuss about *ujamaa* before?"

"It's important that I have a bank account and save my money," Clyde replied softly, then rested his head on his mother's shoulder.

"I have a bank account, too," Jason added. "I've got a hundred dollars!"

He said it like it was a million dollars, and everyone at the table chuckled. Jason smiled brightly.

Collette couldn't help thinking that BriAnne, Clyde and Jason didn't know how lucky they were. They had the love of their parents—their true parents.

But with that thought came a sudden pang of guilt.

In every way that mattered, hadn't Judy and Victor Jenkins been her true parents? They'd raised her, fed her, clothed her, educated her. That's what parents did, didn't they? How many men out there had fathered children yet weren't a part of their lives? Just because they'd donated sperm, did that make them parents?

No.

Still, Collette felt confused.

In her heart, she felt betrayed. That's what hurt the most, that the family she had loved unconditionally had never told her the truth. And now that she was alone in the world, the fact that she had a mother and father and possibly a host of siblings and other relatives out there was something that gave her hope. Maybe she would have a family again.

But was wanting to reunite with her birth family a betrayal to the family she'd known?

"Can I talk about *ujamaa* now?" BriAnne asked.

"Okay, BriAnne," Dexter replied. "Go ahead."

As BriAnne made her way to the head of the table, Collette glanced to her left and saw Nadine staring at her. Nadine smiled.

Collette had noticed that whenever she glanced Nadine's way, the woman had been looking at her. Collette wondered why.

The question must have registered on her face, for Nadine said, "I know, I keep staring. It's just that you remind me of someone."

Collette didn't get to ask whom, because BriAnne loudly cleared her throat. She held a sheet of paper before her.

"Like my uncle Dexter said," BriAnne began, "*ujamaa* means cooperative economics. My family honors *ujamaa* by helping me with my homework so I can do well in school. If I do well, I can become a doctor. And when I'm a doctor, I will work in our community to help out our people.

"There are several African-Americans who practiced *ujamaa* in the past and many who practice it today. Reverend Jesse Jackson is an example of someone who promotes *ujamaa*. As well as being a reverend and a spokesperson for blacks, he created Operation PUSH. This organization tries to get business corporations to invest money in inner cities. Because of this program, many of these businesses have provided jobs to African-Americans. With good jobs, African-Americans can support their communities by buying goods and services from African-American businesses. Reverend Jesse Jackson is an example to us all, and proves how much we can accomplish with some effort."

BriAnne grinned, indicating that she'd finished her speech. Everyone clapped.

"Thank you, BriAnne." Dexter hugged her. "What a great job."

When BriAnne returned to her seat, Dexter said, "I leave you all with a final thought. Remember, every dollar counts. Spend your money well. We all reap the rewards when we work together. Now, let's eat!"

Collette went to work in the kitchen, helping Dexter with the food. She popped a plate of chicken into the microwave, then fetched juice from the fridge. Rita placed Styrofoam cups on the table, while Nadine did the same with paper plates.

"Ujima," Collette whispered proudly to Dexter. "Collective work and responsibility."

"Mmm hmm."

Collette didn't fix a plate of food for herself until everyone else was provided for. There was plenty of food to go around, and lots of laughter and chatter to go with it.

As she ate, Collette listened to Rita and Nadine discuss the various black-owned businesses in their community. Like her, the two women vowed to do more to support such businesses.

Across the table, Dexter and Blair spoke. With the sound of Rita and Nadine speaking beside her and the children's voices, Collette couldn't make out what they were saying. But it was mesmerizing to watch Dexter speak. Even without understanding him, it was apparent that he was very passionate.

He was passionate about a lot of things. He'd been passionate about basketball. He was obviously passionate about children.

And he'd once been passionate about her.

Maybe he was right. Maybe they had been too young. Would their relationship have survived the natural growing pains from adolescence to adulthood? She'd believed it could have, but maybe she was fooling herself.

The bottom line was that being here with Dexter again was making her remember their friendship.

With their breakup, they'd let that die, too. Collette didn't want that to happen again.

Dexter must have felt her staring, for he suddenly turned to her. His eyes lit up with a smile. He held her gaze for several seconds, and for Collette, it seemed like time had actually stopped.

Her stomach fluttered. Why oh why was she still drawn to him?

Perhaps because she hadn't had a serious relationship since their breakup. Perhaps because the few flings she'd had over the years had failed to compare to what she'd shared with Dexter.

Blair said something Collette didn't hear, and Dexter finally turned back to him.

He's a good friend, she thought, realizing that her attraction to him no doubt stemmed from that friendship. His good looks made her pulse race and his giving nature touched her heart.

Yes, he was a good friend. She didn't want to do anything to jeopardize that.

". . . who she looks like."

Those words penetrated her subconscious, and Collette once again faced Rita and Nadine.

"I'm just telling Rita that you really remind me of someone," Nadine explained.

Examining her face closely, Rita shrugged. "I don't know."

"Maybe someone who comes into the salon . . ." Nadine's voice trailed off as her forehead scrunched.

Collette was mildly disappointed. But why should she be? Was this how she would react every time someone said she reminded them of someone? People had done it for years and it had been no big deal. Everyone looked like someone. The fact that Nadine was probably referring to a woman she'd met once or twice—someone not related to Collette—shouldn't disappoint her.

Picking up a piece of chicken, Collette told herself not to ruin tonight's experience with thoughts of her personal dilemma. Tonight, she simply wanted to savor all that Kwanzaa meant.

After she finished eating, Collette brought her plate to the garbage. She returned to the table, picked up a couple of empty casserole bowls and brought them to the sink. Then she gathered dirty utensils.

The rest of Dexter's guests were still discussing some topic or another, so Collette occupied herself washing dishes. Helping to clean up made her feel as much a part of this family gathering as sipping from the unity cup during the Kwanzaa ceremony.

Umoja—unity. *Ujima*—collective work and responsibility. She liked those principles.

Collette jumped when she felt two arms encircle her waist. The touch was familiar, and even in a crowd of a million people, she'd know it was Dexter's.

"You don't have to do this," he said.

"I want to."

When he let his hands linger on her waist, her heart pounded against her ribcage. God, was there nothing she could do to resist this man? Dexter had said he would wait until she found her mother before pursuing a relationship with her. But at the rate he was going, they'd be in bed before the last guest was gone.

Suddenly Dexter stepped away from her, and when Collette looked around, she realized why. Nadine had appeared.

As Dexter walked away, he held her captive with his eyes, as if to say that although they'd been interrupted now, they would pick up where they left off later. When he finally turned, Collette followed his movements, taking in his smooth, powerful stride and the muscles that bunched and contracted beneath the T-shirt he wore.

The man was too sexy for his own good. Yet he didn't seem to know it.

The sound of splashing water drew Collette's attention to Nadine. "Need some help?" Nadine asked.

"No. I can handle it."

Collette expected the woman to walk away, but she didn't. A fist balled against her lips, Nadine looked to be deep in thought. The puzzle of who Collette reminded her of was no doubt eating at her.

Collette left the woman to her thoughts and returned to the task at hand. She tucked a stray hair behind her ear, then reached for the dish soap.

Out of the corner of her eye, Collette saw Nadine make a half-turn, like she was going to walk away. But then she paused, turned back, and faced Collette once more.

"Do that again," she said.

Collette flashed her a quizzical look. "Do what?"

"Put your hair behind your ear."

Nadine narrowed her eyes, concentrating hard.

Collette did as she asked. She shook her head, loosening the strands of her shoulder-length black hair, then tucked them back into place.

"That's it." Nadine clapped her hands together. "I know who you remind me of. Shaylee." A smile broke out on Nadine's face. "Shaylee Simon."

An eerie sensation passed over Collette, causing goosebumps to pop out all over her skin. The groundskeeper's words suddenly echoed in her mind.

Might be somethin' like Sheryl. Maybe Sherry.

Shaylee.

Oh my God.

Ten

"Shaylee?" Collette asked.

"Shaylee Simon. I knew I'd figure it out sooner or later."

Collette gripped the edge of the sink. "Who's Shaylee Simon?"

Nadine's proud smile at figuring out the mystery faded, replaced by a puzzled frown. "What do you mean who's Shaylee? Aren't you . . . aren't you her daughter?"

Collette could barely catch her breath. "Her daughter?"

"Weren't you raised in Minnesota?"

"No, I was raised in Miami."

Nadine's frown deepened. "Hmm. If you weren't raised in Minnesota . . . I would have sworn . . . You look exactly like her." She shook her head. "Guess I shouldn't jump to conclusions." Pausing, Nadine blew out a sorrowful breath. "Poor Shaylee. Such a shame what happened to her."

Too stunned to react Collette could only stand and stare, speechless.

A phone rang. Or was the ringing in her ears? No,

the ringing must have been real, for Nadine lifted a cell phone to her ear.

Collette's mind was processing everything in slow motion. Nadine's voice sounded distorted as she spoke, and Collette didn't make out what she was saying.

I would have sworn . . . You look exactly like her.

Nadine was turning, walking away.

No. Wait. Collette heard the words in her, but they weren't reaching her lips.

"I've got to go." Nadine's voice didn't sound distorted anymore. "My husband's waiting outside."

Near the door, Rita hugged Nadine. "All right. Thanks for coming."

Nadine waved at Collette.

Why couldn't Collette move? She was literally frozen to the spot as her body shook from the realization that she'd just learned her mother's name.

You look exactly like her.

You sure are a dead ringer for her.

Shaylee Simon.

It was too close to be a coincidence. And in her heart, in her soul, it felt right.

The door closed. Nadine was gone.

No! Collette fought with all her strength to quell her body's trembling, fought to get her legs moving. One step, two. Too slowly.

Too late.

Arms wrapped around her, enfolding her in an embrace. "Collette, my God. What's wrong?"

Her breath came in heavy pants. "That . . . She said . . ."

"I'm not following you."

Collette was instantly aware that Rita and Blair were regarding her with concern. "I . . . I'm not feeling well."

"What—the food?"

Collette nodded. "Yeah. Must be." With Rita and Blair watching, this was not the time to tell Dexter the true cause of her distress. "I'm gonna go."

"I'll go with you."

Collette didn't argue. "See you again, Rita. Blair." She waved to the children.

"I'm sorry you're not feeling well," Rita said.

"Check the leftovers," Dexter told Rita. "See what's spoiled."

Collette opened the door and stepped into the cool night air as Dexter spoke to his cousin. She inhaled deeply, but it didn't make her feel better. Clutching her stomach, she prayed she didn't pass out.

Shaylee Simon.

As she scrambled to her house, she dug the key out of her jeans' pocket. But try as she might, she couldn't slip it into the lock. Damn, why couldn't she get her hands to stop shaking?

A hand covered hers. Dexter's.

"Here. Let me."

Looking up, she let him take the key from her. A second later, she heard a click as the lock turned.

Collette paused only a moment before moving forward, but her legs wobbled, and she faltered.

Dexter reached for her. He caught her and held her up in his strong arms. Her breasts pressing to his chest, she could feel the wild beating of his heart. It matched her own.

Dexter ran his hands down her arms, as if to steady her, then took a step backward. "Collette, I'm sorry. I don't usually keep meat more than two days. I don't know why I didn't throw out the leftover chicken."

"It's not the food."

"What? You think you're coming down with something?"

"Nadine . . ." Collette swallowed, but it didn't dislodge the lump in her throat. "She told me my mother's name."

For a good five seconds, Dexter stared at Collette as they stood in the dimly lit hallway of her home. The firm set of her jaw and her unblinking eyes told him she was certain about what she'd just said. But Dexter was having trouble making sense of this. How on earth would Nadine know Collette's mother's name? She didn't even know Collette or the circumstances of her birth and subsequent adoption. Until a few days ago, Dexter himself hadn't known. And he certainly hadn't told anyone.

"Shaylee." Collette's voice was a mere whisper.

There were too many pieces of this puzzle scattered all over the place. "Hold up, Collette. Back up. *Nadine* told you your mother's name?"

"She'd been looking at me strangely all evening. She told me that I reminded her of someone. Finally, she remembered who. She said I looked like someone named Shaylee Simon."

Processing the info, Dexter paced a few steps to the right, then turned and retraced his steps to the left. "All right. You say she told you that you look like someone named Shaylee. But that doesn't mean—"

"Yes, it does. Dexter, I *know*. I can't explain it, but it feels right. Remember the man at the church? The groundskeeper? He said he thought I looked like someone named Sherry or Sheryl. Now, Nadine says the name Shaylee? Dexter, she thought I was this woman's *daughter*. This can't be a coincidence. It can't."

Dexter looked into Collette's eyes and saw the hope. For that reason, he didn't express his doubt. This seemed too convenient, way too coincidental.

But then, life was stranger than fiction. Nadine was in her early to mid forties. Which would be about Collette's mother's age, assuming she'd been a teenager when she'd given birth.

The pieces of the puzzle were rearranging, fitting together in a bizarre yet plausible way. Maybe this was the clue they needed.

"Shaylee Simon." A smile wavered on Collette's lips. "She could be my mother."

"Wow," was all Dexter could say.

Collette's smile disappeared as quickly as it had formed. "There was one thing that didn't make sense. She asked me if I was raised in Minnesota. I wasn't . . ." Squeezing her forehead, Collette groaned her frustration. "If she'd said any other name than Shaylee . . . Dexter, I have to talk to Nadine. I was too stunned to ask her any questions, but if she knew my mother . . . I have to find out everything she knows about Shaylee."

Thoughts tumbled in Dexter's brain. "I have a better idea."

"You do?"

Dexter nodded. "I brought one of the school's laptops home ever the holiday. It has Internet access. I know you can do people searches over the internet."

"Oh, Dexter." Collette folded her hands before her face as if in prayer. "What a great idea."

Seeing her so happy stirred something inside him. Exactly what, Dexter wasn't sure. All he knew was that he wanted to reach out and touch her, stroke her face, assure her everything would be okay.

His thought became an action.

As his hand palmed her cheek, the happiness disappeared from her eyes, replaced by something else. He couldn't read the exact emotion, but he sensed she was torn.

Slowly, she raised her hand, rested it over his. So she felt it too, this energy between them. How could she not, if what he was feeling was so strong?

There's chemistry between us, Collette. I felt it from the first moment I saw you again. Tell me you feel it too.

Curling her fingers around his hand, Collette carefully removed it from her face.

And Dexter's stomach dropped to his knees.

"Dexter, I already told you . . ."

He nodded brusquely. "Yeah. You did."

She looked at him a moment longer, like she wanted to say something else. She even opened her mouth, but all that escaped was a sigh.

It was better this way, better that she not voice the protests his heart didn't want to hear.

* * *

Collette went to Dexter's house the next morning. It was shortly after ten when she walked up to his door, later than she'd planned to start the internet search, but since arriving in Miami, between anxiety over her true identity and thinking about Dexter, she'd hardly had any sleep. But last night, sleep had finally caught up with her. Thankfully. Now, she felt refreshed and reenergized for the next stage of her search—locating her mother now that she had a name.

Collette inhaled the cool morning air, then exhaled it slowly. The scent of the rich earth filled her nose. It was something she missed, she realized. The air wasn't quite as fresh and invigorating in New York.

Collette knocked on the door and was surprised when Dexter answered almost immediately, like he'd been standing there waiting for her.

"Morning," he said, greeting her with a boisterous voice.

"Good morning."

He held the door open, his eyes lazily perusing the length of her body. "Come in."

Dexter's eyes left a swath of heat along her body. He was dressed in black—black jeans, black tank top. The sight of his well-sculpted golden-brown arms suddenly brought a memory of a night many years ago, a night when she had giddily fallen into those beautiful arms the moment he'd opened the door for her. His mother hadn't been home, and they'd quickly gone to his bedroom.

"*I'll never get enough of you, sweetness.*"

"*Oh, Dexter. I'll never get enough of you.*"

Collette's heart fluttered at the recollection. Why should it come to her now? Collette shook her head, trying to toss the unwanted sexual memory from her mind.

She had to remember why she was here. Dexter's suggestion that they search for her mother via the internet made sense. She was grateful he offered her the use of his laptop since she didn't have one of her own.

She was both excited and scared. In just four days, she'd learned her mother's full name. Now, hopefully, she'd find a way to locate her.

"Well, come in."

She did. The Kwanzaa decorations were still everywhere, but Collette didn't see any sign of a computer.

The feel of Dexter's fingers brushing her neck startled her; then she realized he was fixing the tag inside her shirt. Still, she trembled at his touch.

"Cold?"

"A little." Though she was far from cold. Being near Dexter, she couldn't help but feel warm.

She pushed that thought aside. She was here to find her mother, not fall into his arms like some lovesick teenager. "Where's the computer?"

"In my bedroom," he replied.

"Your bedroom?"

"It's got to reach the phone jack. If I brought it out here, we'd have to hover over the kitchen counter. But there's a desk in my bedroom, which is close to the jack."

"I see." Collette was tempted to ask if he had an extension cord, but thought better of it.

Dexter took her hand. It was warm and moist, and she wondered if he was nervous—nervous the way he'd been the first time he'd brought her to his room.

He led her down the hallway to his bedroom. Just nights ago when they'd entered this room, passion had engulfed them.

And then his ex-wife had called. . . .

"Relax, sweetheart. I'm not going to bite you." His voice startled her out of the memory. "Not unless you want me to."

"Dexter . . ."

"Sorry. Bad joke."

Collette extracted her hand from his. This was exactly the kind of talk she didn't need while working in close quarters with him. Which is why she'd gotten up this morning and drafted a few "rules." She'd told herself she would only mention them if she had a reason, and she'd just been given one.

"That's all good," she told him, moving toward the desk where the laptop rested. She trailed a finger along the black case. "But it reminds me that we should set a few ground rules before we begin."

He walked toward her. "What kind of ground rules?"

"These." She extracted a sheet of paper from her back pocket. "I took the liberty of writing down a few things that came to mind." She handed him the list.

He scanned it, his forehead scrunching with each

passing second. "This isn't a few things. You've got nine items here."

"It should cover all the situations we might . . . find ourselves in."

His eyes widened as he continued to read. "No *accidentally* brushing my hands on yours? What's that supposed to mean?"

Collette snatched the list. She'd hoped he would simply read it, see her concerns, but make no comments. Of course, that had been wishful thinking.

"All right. These are . . . my thoughts." She began to read. "One: no kissing. Two: no touching. Three: no pressure to touch or kiss. Four: no telling me you think I'm beautiful or anything else suggestive. Five: no *accidentally* brushing your hands on mine. Six: don't do that thing where you lean too close to my ear and whisper." *Like you did the other night!*

"Why not?" he interjected.

"Because I don't like it."

He shot her a dubious look. "I think you do."

In fact, it was precisely because she *did* like it that she wanted him to refrain from doing it. His hot breath against her ear the other night had been her undoing. But she pretended to be unfazed by his claim and said, "Can I finish?"

He frowned, but said, "Go on."

"Seven: no suggestive eye movements."

"Suggestive eye movements?"

"You know what I'm talking about, Dexter," Collette said, irritation evident in her voice. She mimicked the way he raised his eyebrows at her when he smiled, which, in the past, had always been a way to let her know he was interested in getting intimate. "That. I don't want to see it while we're working together."

"What else?" he said glumly.

"Eight: no supportive pats on the back or running your hands through my hair."

"That's two things."

"All right. It is. Ten then. No telling me that you want me, how much you regret hurting me in the past, or anything that doesn't have to do with finding my mother."

"That's three things."

"Whatever." She stuffed the list into his palm. "Are we clear?"

He blew out a breath that sounded suspiciously like a huff. "This is going to be torture."

"Exactly," Collette stressed, giving him a rubber smile. "You helping me has to be about my mother. Nothing more."

"Because you're not interested in a relationship with me?"

"I've already told you that."

He shrugged. "You have, but what doesn't make sense is that if you're not interested in me, why the stringent rules? You should be unaffected by my charm, shouldn't you?"

Should be, but for some reason, she wasn't. However, she didn't want to admit that. "The point is I don't want to cloud the issue."

"Sure," he mumbled. When she gave him an indignant look, he added, "You ready to get started?"

She nodded, then stepped aside so Dexter could sit at the desk.

"Oh, I guess you'll need a chair. Sitting on my bed might break one of your rules."

Collette raised an eyebrow when he glanced at her, but ignored him. He left the bedroom, and minutes later returned with a chair from the kitchen table. He placed it beside his, but left a huge gap between the two chairs. He took a seat in front of the desk, opened the laptop and turned it on. Only when the screen flashed to life did Collette sit beside him.

"Just give me a second." He typed information into the computer. He was quick, faster than she would have imagined. Collette watched, but she didn't understand a thing. She had to be the last person left in the world who didn't know a thing about computers.

A weird sound came from the computer. "What's that?"

"That's the sound of the phone line connecting to the Internet." Dexter clicked more keys. "All right. Nadine said your mother's name was Shaylee?"

"Shaylee Simon."

"We don't have a middle name."

Collette's heart suddenly fluttered. "Do I need that?"

"Not necessarily, but the more you have, the better."

Collette watched as he punched the information into a spot on the screen. "What's that?"

"This is a screen where I'm inputting information so it can do a search."

"What are you searching for, exactly?"

"I'm not sure I'll find anything this way, but if your mother has a Web site, it's possible to find it through a search engine."

"I doubt she will."

"So do I, but I don't want to rule anything out."

Collette nodded. She could understand that logic.

Dexter continued to type, then finally announced, "No matches for Shaylee Simon, and I tried a few variations on the spelling. But there are some Simon web sites. What do you think? Is your mother an exotic dancer?"

Collette was thrown by the question, and Dexter must have realized that, for he added, "It's one of the sites listed . . . forget it."

Collette narrowed her eyes disapprovingly as she looked at Dexter, but she smiled. She didn't think she would smile at such an inappropriate comment, but perhaps she had been a little too stressed lately and needed his brand of humor.

He turned back to the computer, using the attached mouse to do things she didn't understand. "Man, there are a lot of pages with Simon in them. Do you want to have a look? Or maybe I could print them and you could check out all the various sites that way."

"Where's the printer?"

"Down there." Dexter pointed to the floor. "I'll attach it if you want me to print some stuff. Which might be the best way to handle this. Then if you see anything you want me to investigate further, I can do that."

"Gosh, I don't know." She didn't have a clue about computers.

"I'll print the pages out, that way you'll have a hard copy of everything. Then, I guess the next step is to check out the white pages online to see if we can locate anyone listed under your mother's name."

"All right."

He typed in the information. "This is letting me check for a Shaylee Simon in all the states. As long as she's listed, that is." He hit more keys, then waited as more information loaded on the screen.

"Why not just check Miami?"

"Because your mother could be anywhere. Didn't you say Nadine mentioned Minnesota?"

"Yes, but . . . I guess I always figured I'd find my mother right here in Miami. Gosh, how silly that sounds now." The thought gave Collette more reason to feel anxious. If her mother wasn't in Miami, how on earth were they going to find her?

"Okay," Dexter said. "Nothing there. Let me just try this."

"What?"

"There's a spot to check for an e-mail address for Shaylee Simon. Nope. Nothing there. But wait, it will let you order a public record." He entered more information. "For a minimum of twenty bucks. What do you think?"

Collette deferred to Dexter. "What do you think I should do?"

"Well, for one, I don't trust giving out credit card info Online."

"Neither do I."

"I say we check other avenues first—like forcing the good old reverend to talk. We can always order a public record if everything else fails."

"I thought this internet stuff was easy. Just put in information and you get what you want." Collette frowned. "This is going to be harder than I thought."

"Not necessarily. She may not be listed under Shaylee. It's not such a common name, so I was hoping we could find something there. Now, I could check for S. Simon, but to do that for all of the U.S. will no doubt give me a gazillion matches. But we can narrow the search significantly by limiting it to Miami. Then I can check Minnesota."

"Okay."

Dexter punched more information into the computer.

"Have you found anything yet?"

"Hold up, Collette," Dexter said. "These things take time."

"Why have I always heard the Internet gives you instant information?"

"Sure, once it's found all the information you've requested. Which can be time consuming. And don't forget, Simon is a common enough name. There are bound to be hundreds, if not thousands, in Miami alone."

"God, she could be anywhere in South Florida. We should probably check Fort Lauderdale, West Palm Beach."

"Not yet. I'll stick with Miami first. But you're right—your mother could be anywhere."

"I know." Collette sighed. "Dexter?"

He turned to her. "Yeah?"

"Thanks for your help." And she meant it. There was no way she could do this alone. "I appreciate it."

"No problem, sweetie."

She let his term of endearment slide.

Eleven

Hours later, all Collette had for her efforts were enough printouts to wallpaper her grandmother's entire house, but no real answers. They had used several different search engines to comb the internet directories. In the end, they'd been on line for over six hours.

"This is nuts," Collette said, then exhaled a frustrated breath. "Worse than trying to find a needle in a haystack."

"Hang in there." Dexter placed a hand on her thigh. Her eyes immediately fell to his hand.

He pulled it away. "Sorry. Rule number three, or is it number four?"

She waved him off. "It's all right." The truth was, his touch had offered her comfort. But realizing Dexter might think she was implying they could forget the rules altogether, Collette added, "I mean, it doesn't matter which rule it is, only that you know you broke one."

"Yeah." Dexter's voice was flat. "Of course." He turned back to the computer. "Don't give up, okay?"

"It's hard, Dexter." There were several S. Simons

and Simons in Miami, and well over one hundred listed in Miami-Dade County. There were three times that number of Simons in Fort Lauderdale and the rest of Broward County, not to mention a whole ton over the states of Florida and Minnesota. Of course, the number of Simons in the continental United States was staggering. Considering her mother could literally be anywhere, the hardest part was trying to figure out what to do next.

Leaning forward, Collette placed her elbows on her knees, then rested her chin on her hands. "Maybe I should just forget about this search and move on."

Dexter whirled in the swivel chair. "What? You mean give up searching for your mother altogether?"

"Maybe."

"Is that what you really want?"

"No." Collette paused. "But what if after all this, my mother doesn't want me? I mean, she could have found me a long time ago if she'd wanted to, couldn't she?"

"Who knows? It's not going to do any good to speculate."

"I guess not."

"I won't tell you that I understand what you're going through, because I don't. But I do know that the difference between those who succeed and those who fail is that those who succeed have faith. *Imani.* That's the seventh principle of Kwanzaa."

"Is it?"

"Mmm hmm. And I have to tell you, Collette. I

think there's a reason that letter was lost in the mail, that you received it just before the Kwanzaa holiday."

Collette gave him a wry grin. "You mean it has nothing to do with the oftentimes incompetent U.S. Postal Service?"

He threw his head back and laughed—a hearty laugh that filled Collette's heart with warmth.

"It's good to see you haven't lost your sense of humor. Humor helps us through a lot of tough situations. That and *imani*. Never lose faith, Collette. No matter the odds, you have to believe it can happen."

It was at moments like this, when Dexter said things that were uplifting and inspiring, that Collette felt a strong emotional pull toward him, not just a physical one. He'd said exactly what she needed to hear, what she needed to believe in the face of nagging doubts that she might never learn the truth.

"Thanks. I needed to hear that."

"Believe it."

Was she wrong to push him away? Collette wondered as Dexter's eyes lingered on her face. His mouth was upturned in a soft smile. Not only was Dexter a good man, he was an attractive one. She couldn't ask for a better combination.

She liked looking at him. His oval-shaped face was a smooth golden brown, with a five o'clock shadow dusting his chiseled jaw line. His dark brown eyes were both striking and sincere, and his smile was genuine. Simply put, he was sexy as hell. So why couldn't she just surrender to him?—let him take her in his arms and make all this pain and frustration go away?

Because it wouldn't go away. This was her reality, whether she liked it or not. Not even the Dexters of the world could solve her problems.

Fleetingly, she wondered if they were spending too much time together. And she wondered what would happen if she stopped fighting her feelings. Would she and Dexter actually have a chance at a future?

She didn't know. But she did know one thing: her list of rules weren't made because she didn't want Dexter's affection, but because she did. She needed to protect herself, for she was vulnerable to him. She didn't want to suffer another heartbreak at Dexter's hands.

Who had broken her mother's heart? Surely someone had; Collette couldn't imagine her mother abandoning her if she'd had love and support.

"Do you want to start making some calls? There are a lot here. We'll no doubt be at it all night."

A sudden thought crossed her mind. "Wait a minute. I forgot about your Kwanzaa celebration. You'll be busy tonight. I don't want to take you away from that."

Dexter shook his head. "I've already decided to cancel it for tonight. I called my family this morning before you came over."

"Oh, no, I can't let you do that . . ."

Dexter cut off her protest with a wave of his hand. "Don't worry about that." His gaze locked on hers, his eyes full of sincere concern, so sincere that her heart raced with the intensity of it. "Some things are more important than celebrating the holidays. This happens to be one of those things. I want to help you, Collette. You need to find your mother."

Guilt swept through her even as she felt a surge of relief. She wanted his help. Finding her mother was no longer a desire, but a very real need. She wasn't sure she could go on if she didn't learn the truth about her past. With Dexter's assistance, she could accomplish the search more quickly. Still, she felt bad about spoiling his holiday.

"So," Dexter began, "where do you want to start?"

Collette looked down at the thick stack of papers in her hands. God, there were so many Simons. If she called them all, it would take several days. "I guess we should start with the ones in Miami. Maybe we could try and figure out which ones are in Perrine. Closest to the church . . ."

"All right. But first, I say we get a bite to eat. I don't know about you, but I'm starved."

"I'm not hungry."

"You have to eat. There's a Jamaican place around the corner. My treat."

"Okay," Collette agreed reluctantly.

The numbers would still be here when they returned.

At *Island Dreams*, Dexter ordered spicy jerk chicken with rice and peas, while Collette ordered a beef roti. They took the food back to Dexter's house, where they could eat and go over the pages of information they'd printed out.

Collette dropped the stack of papers she'd been

examining on the table beside her plate. "God, my eyes are starting to blur."

"Sure sign that you should take a break."

"I can't afford to take a break, Dex."

"The information's not going anywhere."

"I'm sure you wouldn't take a break if it were your mother."

"Is that what you really believe?"

Collette suddenly felt exasperated, drained. "I'm sorry."

He gave her a pointed look. "I promised to help you, didn't I? I'm doing as much for you as I would for my own family."

"And just why is that?" She was picking a fight, she knew, but she was powerless to stop herself, just as she was powerless to determine the outcome of her search. She was so frustrated. "You've spent the whole day helping me . . ."

"I thought you wanted my help."

"I do."

"Then what's the problem?"

"The problem, Dexter, is that . . . I don't know what you really want."

He was silent for a moment, clearly perplexed. "We talked about this already. I told you, whatever's gonna happen between us, we'll discuss when this is over."

"And that's why you're helping me? So I'll feel obligated to you?"

"No." Dexter stared at her. "Damn it, Collette. Why are you doing this?"

She couldn't answer that question. All she knew

was that she'd fueled a fire that wasn't ready to be put out. "Did you fight to save your marriage?"

"Why does that matter?"

"It matters, Dex."

"I tried to make it work, if that's what you mean. But when it became apparent—"

"Yet you didn't try to make it work with me."

He stood and ran a hand over his hair. "I already explained that."

"Maybe, but I still don't understand."

Dexter blew out a frustrated breath. "I can't change the past, Collette. All I can do is try to learn from my mistakes."

"I was a mistake."

"Did I say that?"

"No, but . . ."

As Collette continued to speak, Dexter tuned out her words. God, but he was tempted to shut her up with a kiss. Instead, he let her talk until she ran out of steam. And strangely, her rambling had him feeling optimistic. First that ridiculous list of rules, now her picking a fight . . . it was obvious she still had feelings for him. If she didn't, she'd shut up, keep eating, then get back to work.

Collette had always been passionate. From her questions about algebra and protests that the formulas didn't make sense, to their heated discussions about social issues, to the way she'd moaned in his arms when they'd made love, Dexter had always been intrigued by her spunk and fire. So now, he was mesmerized by the way she put her whole body into her words, even though he was no longer listening to what she was saying.

"Can I get you more juice?" he asked when she finally stopped.

"Juice? Dex, did you hear a word I said?"

"Not really."

"You're impossible."

"*I'm* impossible?"

The corners of his mouth curled as he smiled at her, and Collette wished she could wipe that smirk right off his face—with a kiss.

How pathetic was that?

Judging by the silly smile that played on Dexter's lips, it was obvious he knew she was full of it.

All that talk gone to waste. Dexter knew it was hot air.

And now he probably believed Collette wanted him more than ever.

Which, she thought with chagrin, was something she couldn't deny.

"Hello," Collette said into the receiver when a man answered at the number she'd dialed. "Is this Edward Simon?"

"Yes." The older man's voice was wary.

Collette felt a nervous prickle on her nape. "Mr. Simon, my name is Collette Jenkins. I—"

"Do you know what time it is?"

It was just after nine P.M., and certainly not a time Collette would have considered too late to call someone. "I'm sorry, Mr. Simon. I realize the time, but this is important. I have something to ask you." She paused and took a deep breath. "Do you know someone by the name of Shaylee Simon?"

"Wrong number," he barked.

As she opened her mouth to speak, the line went dead. She slammed the receiver back onto its cradle. Sinking into the sofa, she emitted a low cry of frustration.

She lowered the pen to the paper to cross out his name, then thought better of it and put a question mark beside it instead. She couldn't eliminate any options.

Though as she stared at the thick stack of papers on the coffee table, she had to wonder if this was all a big waste of time. She had called almost thirty numbers and had reached a dead end with every one.

It will only be one, she could hear Dexter say, though he wasn't with her. She suddenly realized how much she wanted him here to give her encouragement as she made the calls. He wasn't, and that was her fault. The atmosphere between them had become strained after the argument she'd started, and Dexter had disappeared to give her space. Just minutes ago, he'd gone to the shower.

If the phone wasn't dead at her grandmother's house, she would have been making the calls from there. Next door, she wouldn't have any distractions.

Like thoughts of Dexter in the shower.

Collette's mind drifted to the sound of running water. She tried to picture Dexter's lean, muscular body naked and wet beneath the jet stream.

Wondering what on earth was wrong with her, she

squeezed her eyes shut to block the image. How did she so easily go from frustration over trying to find her mother to feelings of desire for Dexter? Surely that wasn't normal.

Inhaling a deep breath, Collette forced herself to think of Dexter fully clothed. She forced herself to remember his talk about *imani*—faith—and how it applied to her life. The Dexter in that memory was the friend she cherished, and in no way a threat to her heart.

But just as quickly as she'd pictured him telling her about *imani,* her mind went back to thinking about him in the shower.

Great. She couldn't keep her priorities straight to save her life.

Lord help her, she must be crazy.

Yeah, that had to be it. Somehow, she'd lost her mind.

Twelve

She felt warm, safe, like she was wrapped in a cocoon of love.

Her mother's love?

Collette stirred, waking. Realized it wasn't her mother. It couldn't be. She hadn't found her yet.

Then why did she feel so protected, so safe?

Was she dreaming?

As she stirred again, she realized the arms around her were real, as was the firm chest pressed against her back.

Dexter.

Closing her eyes, she fought the sudden tears. Dexter, always there for her.

Last night, after Dexter had gotten out of the shower, Collette had continued making calls. After an hour, she hadn't found her mother, and the frustration and anxiety of the day had gotten to her, finally bringing her down. Dexter could have told her to go home and get some rest, but instead he'd suggested they take a break to celebrate Kwanzaa, just the two of them. He wanted her to feel hopeful once again.

Dexter had led her to the Kwanzaa table, where he'd passed her the lighter. "Do you remember what the candles stand for?" he'd asked her.

"The black one stands for our people," Collette had replied. "The red for the struggles and hardships we have endured. The green . . ." She shook her head. "I don't remember."

"Green stands for hope. Today we light the first four candles, plus the next green one." When Collette made no move to light the candles, Dexter said, "Go on. Light the candles. Light the black one first."

Collette sighed. She didn't want to do this. She wanted to take two aspirin and curl up under the covers of her bed. Given the fact that she didn't particularly feel in a Kwanzaa mood, she felt it would be hypocritical to light the candles.

"Maybe you should do this, Dex."

"No. You're going to do it."

Collette flicked the lighter on and lit the black candle.

"Now the red one next to it." Collette did as instructed. "Then the green one beside the black one. Good, now, light the next red one. And finally, the next green one."

Collette held the flame over the green candle that was being lit for the first time.

"Hope," Dexter whispered as Collette turned to face him. "Now, today's Kwanzaa principle is *nia*, which means purpose. Our purpose as African-Americans is to restore our race to its traditional greatness."

"Dex, I'm really not feeling up to this."

"Africans began the first communities in the world." Dexter continued as though he hadn't heard her. "But years of slavery made us forget that we'd once been kings and queens. Practicing *nia* will help African-Americans be the best that we can be and never settle for less.

"It's only the two of us here, so I won't bother to discuss some of the blacks who have practiced *nia*. Instead, I'll apply *nia* to our situation. You could live the rest of your life never knowing who your mother is, and there's no reason you can't have a good life, but something will be missing. So, the search for your mother has a specific purpose—to fill a void in your life by giving you the answers about your past. It's only in knowing where we came from that we can go forth as whole people. I understand that, Collette. Which is why I'm behind you all the way. Because I know that once you find your mother, you will feel complete, and in feeling complete you will become the best person you can be. And that's *nia.*"

"Oh, Dex." Dexter's words were so beautiful, they touched Collette in a special place way down in her soul. Her headache was gone. And again, by celebrating Kwanzaa with her, even in this small way, he'd given her more reason to carry on.

Nia.

After that, Collette had felt rejuvenated, and she'd continued going through numbers, circling the ones with Perrine area codes. But at some point she must have become tired and fallen asleep.

It was morning now, and she was in Dexter's bed,

securely wrapped in his arms. He must have carried her to his bedroom after she'd fallen asleep.

It would be so easy to let go and fall for him again. But still, Collette was afraid. Especially after what Dexter had said about *nia*. How could she go on, plan a future, get married even, when she didn't truly know where she came from?

"You awake?" Dexter asked softly.

"Yeah." Lifting her head, she craned her neck to see the clock over his shoulder. The digital clock read seven-eighteen A.M.

"You want to get up now?" Dexter's question ended on a yawn. "Get back to work?"

"If you're tired . . ."

"I'll be fine."

Dexter pulled his arms from around her waist and sat up, taking with him the warmth of his body. Following his example, Collette sat up. She finger-combed her flat hair. "All right then. I just want to go back to my place and take a shower."

"Okay. I'll fix some breakfast for when you come back."

"You don't have to," Collette said, standing.

Dexter gave her a look that said he wasn't going to argue with her. "Scrambled eggs okay?"

A smile touched Collette's lips. Dexter was stubborn, but he was also right. They needed to have breakfast before they started to work again. "Sure."

"There. That was easy."

"See you in a little while."

* * *

Dexter was bent over stretching when he heard the front door fly open and hit the wall just minutes after Collette had left. Seconds later, she charged into his bedroom, her breathing ragged, as if she'd run a marathon.

Or as if someone had chased her.

Dexter immediately shot to his full height and took in her appearance. Her lips were trembling; her eyes were wide and terror-filled.

His protective instinct took over, and he was instantly at her side. His hands ached from the urge to touch her, but he remembered her silly rules.

"Collette, what happened?"

She thrust a crumpled envelope and piece of paper at him. "Th-this was . . ." She stopped, swallowed. ". . . stuck in my door."

Dexter unfolded the sheet of paper and immediately saw the reason for her distress. In big bold letters someone had written:

YOU ARE THE DEVIL'S WHORE, JUST LIKE YOUR MOTHER!

IF YOU VALUE YOUR LIFE, GO BACK TO WHERE YOU CAME FROM.

YOU'RE NOT WELCOME HERE.

Dexter checked the envelope for a clue. It held none. It hadn't even been addressed to a specific person. "This was in the door?"

"Yes."

"This sounds like . . ." Dexter stopped short,

frowning. "This sounds like what that crazy woman said to you at the church Friday night."

She managed a jerky nod. "Dexter, do you think an old woman would actually write something like this and bring it to my house? What does that mean? Why would she threaten my life?"

"I don't know." Dexter smacked the envelope and letter against his thigh. "All I know is that this letter is more proof that someone has something to hide. So far, all clues lead back to the church. This is connected to the reverend, no doubt about it."

"That old lady must know who I am, who my mother is. From what she said to me, I figured as much. Either that or she's simply nuts."

"Oh, she's definitely nuts . . . but she knows you. I'd bet money on it." Dexter's forehead wrinkled as he tried to make sense of the situation. "She got into the car with Jabari. Maybe they're related."

"Oh, God." Collette's eyes lit up. "Dex, what if you're right? Oh, that makes sense. If Jabari and that woman are related, then that means she's related to the reverend."

"Reverend Evans. It all comes back to him."

"Who knows if the old lady really wrote this note?"

"Or if the reverend did, trying to throw you off."

"What is it that he doesn't want us to know? Why is he being so secretive?"

"That's what we have to find out."

Dexter watched Collette hug her torso as she paced the hardwood floor, wishing it could be his arms around her instead.

Stopping, she faced him. "I was thinking about

something last night. About the reverend and why he doesn't want to tell me what he knows. Dex, I haven't found the adoption papers, and now I'm starting to wonder if I ever will.

"Maybe there's something shady behind my adoption and the reverend took part in it? The baby was left at his church." Something tickled at Collette's consciousness, a thought she couldn't quite grasp. Like a couple of days ago, she had the feeling that she was missing something important. "This all happened twenty-seven years ago. A lot of teenage girls gave up their babies back then, and who knows if the courts played a part in all of those adoptions? Lawyers set up private adoptions." This was making sense— and leaving more questions to be answered. "What if some shady lawyer handled my adoption? That would explain why my parents never told me."

Dexter looked at her thoughtfully. "And if the reverend was involved, it might explain what he has to hide. I think you're on to something."

"It's Sunday. We have to go to the church."

Dexter shook his head. "I'm not sure that's such a great idea, especially in light of what you've just come up with."

"I think that's even more reason . . ."

"Wait." He held up a hand. "Hear me out. The note you received is a direct threat. A warning to stay away. There's a reason you got it this morning, just hours before church service is to start."

"Which is exactly why I have to go there and show my face. The reverend fears I'm getting close to the truth, and if he realizes it's only a matter of time, he might crack under pressure."

"That's exactly what I'm afraid of, Collette. No," Dexter reiterated, "I think going to the church this morning is a bad idea. One, the reverend's probably going to be expecting you—he might not even be there. But it's also New Year's Eve tonight. Churches always have some type of service to commemorate the passing of the old year. So . . ." Dexter paused, thinking. "So, if he doesn't see us this morning, or if word gets back to him that we didn't show, he'll probably think you've heeded his warning to stay away. And he'll have no reason not to show up for the church's New Year's Eve gathering."

"You think so?"

Dexter nodded. "Not only that, I'd like to spend the day finding out what the reverend is hiding. Maybe locate more articles about Baby Jane, any statements he may have made to the press that contradict what he's been telling us. I hope we can find that info over the internet." Dexter paused. "And in the process, if we find your mother, there'll be no reason to go back to the church—and no reason for anyone to try and hurt you."

Collette inhaled deeply as she regarded Dexter. Her eyes said she agreed with him. "You're probably right."

"I think this is the best way to proceed. If we come up empty after today, then we'll go to the church tonight and make him give us the answers we want."

"Okay. But what about Kwanzaa, Dex?"

"What about it?" he asked rhetorically. "Like I said

yesterday, finding your mother is more important. And given that note, I'm not about to leave you to do it alone."

Collette gave him a grateful smile. "Don't you have to call your family and tell them you won't be here again tonight?"

"Actually, this is the night of the *karamu.*"

"The what?"

"*Karamu.* That means feast. The sixth night of Kwanzaa is when the biggest celebration is held. The day's principle is *kuumba,* which means creativity. The festivities will be held at the school tonight. It's open to the entire community—all races. Anyone who wants to can come and enjoy it. In keeping with the principle of creativity, we're having African dancers, live music, an art display. And of course, lots of food. Jeremy's really excited—he and a few friends have learned to play the congas and they'll perform for an audience for the first time tonight. We want everyone to come and enjoy what Kwanzaa is all about, and hopefully, be inspired to celebrate it with their own families if they aren't already."

"You helped plan this night." Collette's voice relayed her pride.

"Mmm hmm. Me and a couple other teachers who celebrate Kwanzaa. If we'd been in touch, I would have invited you to display your artwork at the celebration. A Miami born and raised African-American artist, making a living by practicing the principle of *kuumba.*"

"I would have liked that."

"You'd be an inspiration to the children."

Collette said, "I admire your commitment to teaching. It's quite obvious you're good with children, that you love your job."

"I do."

Collette sat on the edge of Dexter's bed. "Whatever happened with your basketball scholarship?"

Dexter shrugged nonchalantly, as if it didn't matter. It didn't—not anymore. Once, he'd dreamed of being an NBA star, but a shoulder injury had sent his life on a different course. "I was pretty good," he said in reply to her question. "Although I always got teased for being one of the shortest guys on the team. Short at six-foot-three. Imagine that." Dexter smiled.

"What happened?"

"I busted my shoulder in junior year and it's never been the same since. I tried playing again in senior year, months after it had healed, but I kept reinjuring it. Long before the NBA draft, I knew I didn't stand a chance of making the cut."

"I'm sorry."

"It's okay. I honestly think I was meant to be a teacher. And I coach basketball at the school, so I still get to enjoy the game in a very real way. It's the best of both worlds."

"The celebration tonight sounds like it will be a lot of fun."

"It should be," Dexter said. "Oh well. Next year."

"I'm sorry, Dex."

"Like I said, it's no big deal."

They fell into silence, Collette staring up at him from her seat on the bed, him staring down at her. And as they stared at each other, something changed.

Collette's deep brown eyes grew darker, almost onyx, and Dexter's groin tightened in response. He didn't know why exactly, except that Collette seemed to be telling him with her eyes what she couldn't say with words.

Hold me, Dex. Love me.

Once, he'd been able to read her body language, her subtle looks and expressions. But years had passed, and in those years they'd grown apart. Now, he couldn't be sure. He remembered all her protests, how she kept pushing him away.

And he remembered that finding her mother had to be paramount. If Dexter mixed business with pleasure before Collette had solved her life's mystery, she would run, not walk, out of his life.

Still, his primal male reaction to her almost made him forget his resolve. He fought that urge, and, breaking eye-contact, turned to the computer.

Dexter busied himself with the task of starting it up, though he didn't know why. He'd already printed out a ton of information, information they should now follow up on.

He turned, and was surprised to find Collette standing over his shoulder. How was it he hadn't heard the bed squeak when she'd gotten up?

"What are you thinking?" she asked.

"I'm thinking we should do an official people search now," Dexter told her. "Yesterday, we had no idea how much information we'd get, and it's going to take forever to follow up on this." Dexter indicated to the stack of printouts. "I know I was wary of giving a credit card number over the Internet, but maybe

I'm just paranoid because of the horror stories floating around. Anyway, there are supposed to be a lot of secure sites, and I suppose a legitimate people-finder site should be secure. We can use my credit card."

"Oh, that's not necessary," Collette said. "But I agree. It'll be quicker if we do the search that way, so let's do it."

As Dexter looked up at Collette, he offered her a comforting smile. "If these guys can deliver on their promise of locating anyone in America, you might be able to find out where your mother is before the new year."

Collette's eyes fluttered shut as she pressed her lips together. When she reopened them, the flame of hope burned bright. "Gosh, to be able to start the new year knowing who my mother is. Maybe even getting to meet her tonight . . ."

Seeing Collette happy with the promise of hope pulled at something inside Dexter, the part of him that knew he would do anything to make her happy, just so he could always see her beautiful smile.

"This might take a while." Dexter stood and gestured to the swivel chair. "You take the more comfortable chair."

Collette didn't protest. She sat on the leather chair and slid it to the left of the desk. Dexter pulled the chair from the kitchen table squarely in front of the laptop and started to type.

"GPM People Finders," he read aloud after bringing up a list of sites that offered services to locate people. "Guaranteed to locate a loved one or friend within half an hour or your money back."

"Wow." Collette stared at the screen. "As convenient as ordering a pizza."

Her humor was back. "Yes, but this will me much more satisfying." Dexter clicked on GPM's hot link, which would take him directly to the site without him having to type in the long internet address. "Okay, let's bring the site up."

Dexter and Collette waited as the site downloaded. A few more keystrokes and an online application appeared. There were several boxes to fill out—person's name, city and state of birth, date of birth, social security number, sex.

"We don't have all that info," Collette pointed out.

"See the red asterisks beside some of the boxes?" Dexter pointed them out.

"Yeah."

"That means those are the only boxes that *need* to be filled out. In other words, that's the minimum amount of information needed to do the search. So, let's see here. It says we need your mother's name, the city where she was born, and the state. And her sex, of course." Dexter typed in the required information. "Let's hope this works. The one thing going for us is that Shaylee isn't all that common a name. I'm sure it was even less so nearly thirty years ago."

"Hmm."

At Collette's brief response, Dexter stole a glance at her. Beside him, she sat hunched forward with reverently folded hands pressed against her lips. So much was riding on this, and Dexter wished he could assure her that everything would go their way. Instead, he said a silent prayer that this search would garner the result she wanted.

He turned back to the computer and hit the enter button on the keyboard to send the information he'd provided. A screen came up that asked for a credit card number.

"Unless you have your credit card here, we may as well use mine."

"I didn't bring my purse," Collette said.

"It's okay. I don't mind using mine." Seconds later, Dexter had his Visa card out of his wallet and was entering it into the computer.

"How much is this costing?"

"It doesn't matter."

"Yes, it does. I'm gonna pay you back. I already owe you so much for helping me."

Dexter met her eyes. "You owe me nothing." The words had a double meaning, and judging by the way her gaze fell to the ground, she got them both.

"Okay, that's it. Now we wait to see what turns up. It might take a while, so what do you say we have that breakfast I promised you?"

"Sure."

Dexter was about to get up when a beeping sound came from the computer. His attention went back to the screen. The words SEARCH SUCCESSFUL flashed in bright blue letters.

"Oh, my God." A nervous breath escaped Collette's lips. "That was fast."

"Tell me about it."

Dexter followed the directions for getting to the

page where the information they sought was listed. Seconds later, it popped up.

"What does it say?" Collette asked.

There was a lot of information, all in fine print, so Dexter skimmed for the crucial information.

"Shaylee Leanne Simon," he read. "Born in the city of Miami, Dade County, Florida, July eighteenth, 1956." Dexter's heart pounded as he read the information. He shot a quick glance at Collette. Her whole body taut, she didn't appear to be breathing. He raised his eyebrows as if to confirm they'd struck gold, then returned his attention to the computer. "July eighteenth, 1956," he reread, finding the place where he'd left off. His eyes went to the next line.

And then he froze, as if his blood had turned to ice.

"What is it, Dex?"

No, not this. Anything but this.

"Dex?"

Unable to say a word, Dexter met Collette's wide-eyed gaze with a grim expression. Panic passed over her features.

Feeling helpless, Dexter watched Collette's eyes dart to the computer screen.

He watched her face collapse as she read the devastating news.

Thirteen

The words on the screen blurred before her eyes. Collette's head swam, and she gripped the arms of the chair, not even realizing she'd pushed herself away from the computer. Away from the awful words that glared at her from the monitor.

Died in Miami on November 15, 1973.

"She's dead." Nausea curled inside her stomach. Collette covered her mouth with a hand, her mind negating the awful words. *No, no.* It couldn't be. How could she come this far in her search, only to learn that her mother was dead?

"Ah, hell." Dexter tipped his head back to look up at the ceiling, as though searching for a reason behind this awful blow fate had dealt.

When he turned to her, his eyes were full of genuine sorrow and concern. Standing, he reached for her and slipped an arm around her shoulders. "Come here." Encircling her in a warm embrace, Dexter pulled her close. She let him, resting her head on his shoulder, taking a deep breath as her mind raced.

Never would she hear her mother's voice or see

her face. Never would she get to know the woman who'd given birth to her. Her search was futile, her efforts in vain. Where did she go from here? Dexter's arms felt strong and secure around her, giving her comfort. A shock wave of emotions wracked through her body. She wanted to lean on him, but couldn't allow herself to. She was alone in the world with no family. She had to accept that fact and learn to stand strong on her own. Because while the hope of seeing her mother face to face was gone forever, her search for the truth was far from over.

Still, for this moment, she allowed herself to lean on Dexter, to accept his comfort and strength as she tried to come to terms with what she'd just learned.

"My God, Dex, what happened to her?" She drew back from his embrace to meet his gaze. Tears threatened to spill from her eyes, but she held them back, forcing the devastating feeling of despair to recede. "I have to know. I have to find out what happened to her."

"Then that's what we'll do. I told you I'd help you, and I meant it. Whatever it takes, we're going to find out what happened to your mother."

Collette stepped away from him. Fighting the need to simply fold herself into Dexter's arms once more, she paced the floor. Her mind raced in ten different directions. "The woman at your house—Nadine—she made some comment about it being a shame what happened to Shaylee—to my mother. At the time, I assumed she meant that it was a shame Shaylee had been an unwed mother. Things were so different back then. But what if she meant something else?"

Dexter ran a hand over his shortly cropped hair. "Maybe she did. Something that people had heard about. Otherwise, how would Nadine know? I think if she was close to Shaylee, she would have placed your face right away."

Collette pressed her fingers against her lips, thinking. "My birth mother was seventeen, Dexter. Her life had barely begun." Running both hands over her hair in an unconscious mimic of Dexter's gesture, she spun on her heel and continued to pace. "Could she have died of complications from childbirth?" An ice-cold jolt of pain shot through her. Was she responsible for her mother's death? "Is that why I was left on the church doorstep?" She stopped pacing and halted in front of Dexter. "Who left me there? If my mother died, then why would someone do that?"

Dexter narrowed his gaze, lost in thought. "I don't think that's it."

"Maybe my father. Maybe he was young, too, and with my mother dead, he didn't know what to do." As the words spilled from her lips, Collette realized how much she wished they were true. That her mother hadn't been pregnant and alone, driven to the desperate act of leaving her at the church because she didn't know what else to do.

"I don't know. That doesn't feel right. I think there has to be something more to it."

A sudden thought crossed her mind. "The obituaries. Would they have printed one in the newspaper? Would it tell anything about how she died?"

"I don't think they normally print cause of death, but maybe." Dexter shrugged. "It wouldn't hurt to look. It's a place to start anyway."

"I could ask Felicity," Collette said. "She works at the library. Surely they have old newspapers on microfiche or something."

Dexter pushed both chairs under the desk. "You do that, and I'll go around to the local newspaper offices and talk to them. See what they have on file." Turning, he fully faced Collette, then reached out and stroked her chin. He let his fingers linger there. "We'll work this as a team. Surely we'll come up with something."

Collette fought the urge to simply jerk away from his touch. She had to focus on what was important, and that was finding out what had happened to her mother.

She couldn't let her attraction to her former flame distract her from her purpose.

Casually, as though his touch meant nothing, she stepped away. "Well, there's no time like the present. I'm going to the library now to see if Felicity can help." She glanced at her watch. "Shall we meet at my house, say sometime this evening, to compare notes?"

"Sure." He shoved his hands in his pockets, as though giving them something to do other than touch her. "How about five, five-thirty? With it being New Year's Eve, everything will probably close up early. I can pick us up some dinner."

Dinner. Such a simple thing, yet Collette's heart raced at the suggestion.

As though reading her mind, Dexter added, "Or does that break one of your rules?"

His lips curved in a slow, sexy grin that had her blood heating, in spite of her resolve to back away from him emotionally. The truth was, he'd already broken most of her rules—and she hadn't minded. "Not really, I guess."

"Good."

"But you don't have to buy dinner, Dex. You've done so much for me already."

"Spending a quiet evening with you over dinner is not exactly a burden, Collette."

She should tell him that his comment was suggestive—a definite no-no according to her rules—but the truth was, she liked it. And she especially liked the way he said her name; it left her toes curling and her palms tingling with the urge to reach out and touch him the same way he'd touched her.

She hid her reaction with a throaty chuckle. "Well, since you put it that way, I can hardly resist. So, five o'clock, right?"

"It's a date." He smiled again, touching her lightly on the back as he guided her through the bedroom door.

Collette shivered. *Stop it*, she told herself. She had to focus on where her priorities lay, and those priorities did not include indulging in fantasies of what it would be like to feel Dexter's hands on her body, with no clothing as a barrier beneath his touch.

"Do you need a ride to the library?" Dexter asked when they were at the front door.

"I'll call a cab."

"I can take you."

"No, that's okay." The last thing she needed was to be in a confined space with this incredibly sexy man.

"You sure?"

"Oh, yes." She gave him a smile she hoped looked real. "I'm definitely sure."

"Collette." Felicity smiled with genuine pleasure. "Hey, girl, it's good to see you." She gave Collette a brief hug. "What brings you to the library on New Year's Eve day?"

"I need your help," Collette said. She darted a furtive stare around the room, taking in the people closest to them. An elderly woman browsed the mystery section a few feet away, and a young man of high school age sat at a table next to a pretty girl, doing more flirting than homework if his body language was any indication.

"Is there someplace we can talk privately?" Collette asked.

Felicity's expression turned serious. Concern shot through her pretty brown eyes, and a frown arched her brow. "Sure hon. What's wrong? Are you okay?"

"Yes and no," Collette answered.

"Let's go back here." With a nod of her head, Felicity gestured to a door marked *EMPLOYEES ONLY*, then led the way.

Once inside the library's back office, Felicity closed the door and pointed to a table on which stacks of files were piled. A single chair stood beside it. "Have a seat. You look like you've seen a ghost. Dexter didn't do something to upset you, did he?"

Collette waved her hand. "No, it's not that." Sinking into the chair, she looked up at Felicity as her friend sat on the edge of the table. "It's my birth mother. She's dead."

"What?"

Quickly, Collette explained how Dexter had helped her search the Internet and how they'd located Shaylee Simons's name.

"I need to find out what happened to her," she finished. Slumping forward in the chair, she rested her forehead on the palm of her hand. "God, Felicity, I can't believe she's dead. After coming this close . . ." She let the words trail off as tears welled in her eyes. "It's just so frustrating."

"I'm so sorry, hon."

"Did you get to ask your parents about Baby Jane? If they knew anything?"

"Yeah, I asked. They remember the initial story, but they're not sure if there were any follow-up reports."

Collette sighed.

"Oh, hon. What can I do to help?"

Brushing her hair from her face, Collette sat up straight. "I was hoping you might have some newspapers from that time period on microfiche. After that Nadine woman's comment, I'm thinking something awful happened to my mother—something that might've made the news."

"Could be." Felicity nodded. "It's certainly worth a try, and actually, we do have old newspapers on microfiche. I'd be more than happy to help you look."

Collette squeezed her friend's hand. "Thank you. It would mean a lot. I've got to start somewhere."

"Then let's get to it." Felicity rose from the table, and together they went back into the main area of the library. "The microfiche files are upstairs."

En route upstairs, Felicity stopped to chat with a colleague. "I'm gonna be busy for a while, Linda. But if you need me, you'll find me in the microfiche room."

The hours melted away as Collette pored over file after file of back issues of the local papers. By the time Linda stuck her head in the door to say she was taking a lunch break, Collette's neck ached and her eyes burned from skimming the dozens of newspaper articles. Frustration gripped her. So far, they had found nothing.

Groaning, Collette smacked her palm against the desktop. "This is going nowhere. What am I going to do if we can't find anything?"

Her frustration reflected in Felicity's gaze. "Don't give up, hon." She glanced at her watch. "But we've been at this for a while and I don't know about you, but my mind is in a haze from looking over all this stuff. Why don't we get a bite to eat? Maybe a little food will help us think more clearly."

Collette rubbed her eyes, not really hungry, but knowing Felicity was right. Her stomach growled, and her head felt light. "Okay. I guess we could both use a break."

Collette left Felicity to take care of some duties that needed tending to, and went to the deli a few doors down from the library. A little while later, she returned with sub sandwiches, chips, and coffee. They went into the back office to eat.

Felicity washed down a bite of her turkey sub with coffee. "You say Dexter is helping you?"

"Mmm hmm."

"How's that going?"

"Well, it's been slow—"

Felicity gave Collette a pointed look. "That's not what I mean."

Collette played dumb. "What *do* you mean?"

"C'mon. Are you gonna tell me that you're not the least bit interested in Mr. Oh-So-Fine Dexter Harris? That you aren't happy to know he's single?"

"Oh, that." Like the thought alone hadn't sent her heart fluttering time and again. "Makes no difference to me."

"Hmm."

Collette sipped her coffee. "What's that supposed to mean?"

"Nothing," Felicity replied in a singsong voice. She reached for the second half of her sub.

"Okay, so he's single again. So he's still fine." Oh, was he fine—lean, sexy body, beautifully sculpted arms. And those lips. "That's all well and good, but I really have no interest in putting my heart on another dart board, Felicity. You of all people should understand that."

"You were practically kids back then. I don't think Dexter . . ."

"Exactly. I was young and stupid. Thought I knew what love was . . ." Her voice trailed off. "I won't make the same mistake twice."

Felicity swallowed another bite, then said, "In that case, doesn't it bother you to work with him?"

Collette contemplated the question as she drank another sip of coffee. "Maybe a little. I appreciate his help, I really do. I don't know where I'd be if he wasn't helping me. But in a way, it's weird."

"Because the chemistry's still there."

"Because we haven't been in touch for years." Collette spoke as if thoughts of her and Dexter getting physical hadn't tumbled through her mind every hour of every day since she'd met him again.

Felicity shook her head. "Sounds crazy to me. After how hot you two were for each other."

Collette was about to bite into her sub, but stopped. "*Were* is the key word. A high school crush. It ended ages ago."

"It was more than that with you and Dexter. Yeah, it was only high school, but you two were inseparable."

"And he ended it," Collette answered quickly, plainly.

"So you're saying you don't feel *anything* for him now? Is that it?"

Since Felicity wasn't about to stop questioning her—and since Collette suddenly found she wanted to talk about it—she decided to speak openly about her feelings. "All right. I'm not gonna lie. He's still sexy as sin—even more so—and yeah, I'm attracted to him. I know he's attracted to me, but after all this time, what can it be? Lust, probably. Or maybe residual feelings. But I'm not seventeen anymore. I'm not about to fall head-over-heels for him again." When Felicity didn't say anything, Collette added softly, "Besides, even if I wanted to pursue something with him, I'm not sure this is the time. Last week, I thought I had my life together. My career was going well, I was dating. Nothing serious, but I was happy. Now, the rug has been pulled out from under me. I know this won't make much sense, but I feel . . . lost. Like I'm suddenly incomplete. And if I'm incomplete, how can I truly be free to love anyone? Worse, how can I get into a serious relationship? I'll never be sure that when I date a guy, I'm not dating a blood relative. A half brother. An uncle. Even a cousin."

"You are not related to Dexter. You know his whole family."

"Okay, so I don't think Dexter and I are related. That doesn't change the fact that I suddenly don't know who I am."

"You know who you are. You're Collette Elizabeth Jenkins. Born and raised in Miami by parents who adored you."

"They weren't my parents."

"How do you figure that?"

Felicity's comment gave Collette pause. She went back and forth on this issue, one moment feeling that the Jenkins *were* her parents—they'd raised her, after all—the next feeling that by keeping the truth from her they'd broken the parent-child bond.

"Hey, hon. I understand this is all a shock, but the

truth is, none of this changes who you are. Who you are is the person you were raised you to be, by the people who were your parents in every way that matters most."

"But what about my passion for art? No one in my family is an artist." Collette sighed. "It would just be nice to know, to really understand, what part my biological parents' genetics played in making me who I am. Like, if I found out my mother loved art . . . I don't know. It would just help me feel . . . feel like I had a piece of her."

They fell into silence, each finishing their lunch. Afterward, Collette and Felicity were back at the microfiche records, Collette more determined than ever to find what she was looking for.

"We've tried all the bigger newspapers," Felicity said. "Maybe we're hunting in the wrong place. Maybe we ought to be searching the smaller papers that were around back then. They'd probably do more coverage on a local story."

New hope lifted Collette's flagging spirits. "I didn't think of that. Were there some?"

"Probably. The church was in Perrine, which is in south Miami-Dade, so let's see what I can find there." Felicity flipped through the microfiche files. A short while later, she said, "Here we go. *The Perrine Daily News* and *South Florida Today* are ones we didn't check yet. You take one, I'll take the other."

Just over an hour later, Collette's gaze fell on the words she'd been seeking, words that caused her heart to jump in her chest. New energy surged through her as the newspaper headline all but leaped out at her from the projector.

WOMAN'S BODY FOUND IN ALLEY.

"Felicity, look at this! Here, I think I've found something."

"What?" Felicity jumped up from her seat to read over Collette's shoulder.

> *The body of a young black woman was found early yesterday morning in an alley behind the First Baptist Church of Perrine on US-1. The victim's identity has not yet been released, pending notification of next of kin.*
>
> *Police declined to comment, stating only that the woman was the victim of a possible homicide.*

A photo of the alley, cordoned off in crime scene tape, accompanied the article. Excitement raced through Collette as she recognized the back door of the church where she and Dexter had spoken to the groundskeeper.

"Do you think it was her?" The sandwich she'd consumed whirled inside her stomach, and for a moment, she thought she might be sick. Had her mother met such a tragic, violent ending—murdered in a back alley?

"Flip to the next day," Felicity said, her tone urgent. "This might be what you're looking for."

Luck suddenly seemed to be with Collette as she

scanned the following day's stories. On page two was a headline highlighted in bold print.

LOCAL DRIFTER QUESTIONED IN HOMICIDE

The body of a young black woman, found dead early Sunday morning in the alley behind the Perrine First Baptist Church, has been identified as that of Shaylee Simons, age seventeen. Simons's roommate reported her missing when Simons did not show up for her shift at the cafe where both women worked as waitresses. The body was discovered by Myron Honeycutt, a local drifter known for doing odd jobs about the neighborhood.

Upon discovering the body, Honeycutt immediately called Reverend Joseph Evans, pastor of the First Baptist Church of Perrine for the past seven years, who contacted police.

Collette's heart lodged in her throat. She read on.

Cause of death is listed as strangulation. Reporters on the scene could get no comment from Simons's roommate, who was taken to the hospital and treated for shock. Evans also declined to be interviewed. However, Myron Honeycutt—who was questioned by police—is quoted as saying, "It's a sad day in our town when a murder is committed right outside the very house of our Lord."

Cold sweat broke out across Collette's forehead as her gaze moved to the sidebar of the article. A photo taken of Shaylee Simons in happier times, possibly a school picture, stared back at her.

Her friend's eyes widened with sympathy and horror.

"Sweet Jesus, girlfriend." Felicity clutched a hand to her heart. "You look just like her. In the eyes . . . and her smile."

An eerie combination of elation at seeing her mother's face for the first time, and sorrow at knowing she would never have the chance to meet her, gripped Collette and wouldn't let go.

She stared at the beautiful eyes looking back at her from the grainy photograph.

Eyes that were a mirror image of her own.

Fourteen

Collette stood at the small window in the kitchen, looking out at Dexter's house. Where was he? She'd hoped he'd be home after she returned from the library—she needed to tell him what she'd found—but his car hadn't been in the driveway. Now, almost an hour later, it still wasn't there.

Letting the curtain fall back in place, she glanced at the clock on the wall for the sixth time in as many minutes. It was just after five. Dexter had said five or five-thirty. She prayed he'd make it home any minute.

It seemed like hours later when she heard the sound of a car pulling up outside, but it was really only minutes. She parted the curtain again. Her heart leaped with anticipation at the sight of Dexter's car.

As he got out of the maroon-colored Saturn, she quickly closed the curtain and took a deep breath.

Get a hold of yourself, Collette. This isn't a date.

But her heart said something else as she opened the door and saw him standing there, holding a bottle of wine.

"Hi." He smiled and held out the bottle. "I would

have been here sooner, but I forgot to pick up some wine, so I stopped to get some."

"No dinner?" Smiling, Collette held the door wide and motioned him in.

"I figured we could rustle something up here. But wine . . ." He raised the bottle. "Well, we can't exactly make some in the backyard. I thought a glass with dinner might help you unwind after your day at the library."

Barely waiting for him to set the bottle down on the coffee table, she spoke. "Never mind unwinding, I think we should drink a toast to my success." A sense of accomplishment warmed her insides, though sadness accompanied it. "I found what I was looking for, though I can't say I'm happy at what I learned."

Dexter frowned. "What is it?"

"Here. See for yourself." Bending over the coffee table, she picked up the copies of the articles Felicity had printed from the microfiche and handed them to him.

Grasping the pages, Dexter sank down onto the sofa, his eyes already skimming the story. When he turned to the next page, his expression mirrored her own surprise at seeing her mother's face.

"There's no question this woman is your mother," he said. He looked over at the article once more, shaking his head. "Strangled outside the very same church where you were left. And I'm sure you didn't miss the fact that our buddy Reverend Evans was called to the scene."

"Not for a minute," Collette said. She glanced at

the bottle of white wine. "I'm not so hungry right now, but I sure could use a glass of that wine. Do you mind holding off on dinner?"

"Not at all." He rose from the sofa and followed her to the kitchen. Collette tried not to notice the way the scent of his cologne drifted her way. For the first time since he'd stepped into her living room, she really looked at him. Dexter was any healthy woman's fantasy. Freshly shaved, his mustache neatly trimmed, he wore black jeans with a white dress shirt, open at the collar, and cuff links—an irresistible combination. Part formal, part casual, all male—looking good and smelling even better.

Forcing herself to get a grip, she focused on the issue at hand. "What do you think of the fact that the police questioned the drifter, Myron Honeycutt?"

Dexter accepted the corkscrew she pulled from a kitchen drawer and worked at opening the bottle of wine. "It says he was questioned and released. I doubt he knew anything of any relevance, or he would've been kept in custody."

"You're probably right." She pulled wineglasses from a cupboard—the glasses her grandmother had used to celebrate special occasions. What secrets had Grandma Kathryn taken to the grave with her?"

"Too bad he's not still around." Dexter took the glasses from her and poured the wine. "But that doesn't leave out the Reverend Evans. He knows more than he's letting on. Hell, he has to. Why else did he faint dead away the moment he laid eyes on you?"

Collette sipped the wine, grateful for its calming

effect. It had been one hell of a day. "Maybe I simply startled him, looking so much like the woman found dead outside his church all those years ago."

"Uh-uh. I'd wager there's more to it than that." Dexter's lips closed over the rim of his glass, his long, strong fingers gripping the stem. He wore a ring made of Black Forest gold, and his nails were clean and neatly trimmed. The urge to reach out and touch him gripped her. He had very sexy hands.

"Wait a minute. What's the date on these articles?" Dexter was up and rushing to the living room before he finished the question. Returning, he once again took his seat. "November sixteenth and seventeenth. When were you left at the church?"

A chill snaked down her spine. "November fourteenth. I remember that because it's ten days after my birthday. Oh my God."

Dexter could only nod his agreement to her inner thoughts. "We're getting close to unraveling this, sweetie."

Sweetie. The word reverberated through her body, leaving it thrumming.

Dexter lifted his glass again. Collette watched as his tongue snaked out to skim briefly over his bottom lip, dispersing a drop of wine. Her own tongue pressed against the inside of her bottom lip, and she stopped just short of actually licking it. God, she wanted to devour his mouth. What the hell was wrong with her? Quickly, she averted her eyes and, willing her thoughts back to her mother, took a sip of her own wine.

Lord, but it's suddenly warm inside this kitchen, she thought.

Rising from her chair, she moved across the room and opened a window.

"You really think this is unraveling?" she asked, making an effort to focus on what Dexter had said.

"No doubt. Like I said, everything keeps coming back to the reverend. The man has something to hide."

"You think . . . you think he could have *hurt* my mother?"

"Who knows?"

"Oh, Dex. I don't know about that. Yes, my mother was obviously killed after she left me at the church, but that could have been by anyone, maybe even a boyfriend. The reverend saw my mother's body. Then he sees her ghost appear at his church years later?"

"Why would he avoid us if he'd simply been startled by the resemblance between you and Shaylee Simon? Why wouldn't he simply acknowledge that?"

"You're right." She sat back down. "Unless, of course, he just doesn't want to stir up old memories of such an unpleasant crime. He's a man of the cloth. Maybe it bothered him more than he cared to admit when my mother's body was found." A thought flickered inside her mind, like a flame fueled by oxygen. "Maybe she was a member of his church. That could possibly explain why her death would upset him."

"Could be. But then, why did the man peel out of the parking lot the other day, driving like Satan in a hot-wired Lamborghini?"

Collette sighed, knowing he was right. She hated

to think that a man of God could be hiding some horrible secret, but what else could it be? There was just no logical reason behind Reverend Evans's behavior.

"Maybe there *was* some shady adoption deal," Collette said after a moment.

The reverend's behavior was certainly suspicious, but what about that creepy old woman, staring at her, calling her names as if she were indeed the spawn of Satan himself? What was that all about?

So many questions. "Do you think Reverend Evans won't talk to us because he's scared to?"

"I don't know." Dexter set his wineglass on the table. "If he played a part in some shady adoption, he could be scared. Or it could be something else he's hiding. Either way, he's no fool. He knows something and he obviously doesn't want us to find out what it is. But tonight we'll head to the church."

Collette let out a shaky breath. "Okay."

"It's not even six yet, so it'll be a long night." Dexter rose and moved over to her chair, reaching out to run his fingers across her cheek. "In the meantime, I want to pamper you a little. You've had a hard day, sweetie."

The endearment rolled off his tongue like hot butter over popcorn.

Collette tensed, fighting the way he made her feel. "So have you," she said.

"Yeah, but you must really be drained emotionally, searching so long and hard, and then finding that article and the picture of your mother." He leaned down and kissed her forehead, and Collette's pulse thundered inside her temple.

"Really, Dex. I . . ."

He cut her off. "Let me make you some dinner. What have you got to work with?" Not waiting for an answer, he turned and made himself at home by opening her refrigerator to peer inside.

Torn between irritation at the bold way he seemed to fall so easily into being a part of her home, and liking the way he looked doing so, Collette moved over to the cupboard beside the refrigerator. "I picked up some groceries today. I've got brown rice and just about any kind of vegetable you'd care to have. And there's chicken. It shouldn't be quite frozen yet, but if need be, we can thaw it in the microwave."

"Sit down," Dexter said, his words so gentle they were more a caress than a command. His sexy lips curved in a soft smile.

Lord help her, she wanted to kiss him.

"I said I'd like to pamper you." He took a pack of chicken breasts from the freezer. "It's easy to see you're a strong woman, Collette. But why don't you let yourself lean on me for a little while; I assure you I won't poison you. I'm a pretty darned good cook." His smile deepened to a grin, and Collette gave in to him, returning to her seat at the table.

Though she hated to admit it, she was starting to enjoy his attention.

"Fine." Collette shrugged, pretending it was no big deal. She smiled, unable to resist teasing him back a little. "You cook, I'll watch. And I'll be the judge of whether or not it's edible."

He made a silly face.

Collette chuckled softly, then picked up her wineglass once more. Getting serious again, she said, "You never did tell me if you found out anything at the newspaper offices."

He looked at her over his shoulder as he sliced a tomato for a salad. "I didn't think to look at the smaller community papers. I found nothing in the bigger ones. But you know what, maybe we can call the police station and see if an arrest was ever made."

"They say if an arrest isn't made shortly after a murder . . ." Collette paused, nearly choking on the word. "It's unlikely one ever will be made. In any case, I checked the papers for three months after that date and found nothing."

"You're probably right."

They shared a comfortable silence while Dexter finished slicing the tomato. Collette watched him go to work making the meal. A short time later, over a dinner of stir-fried chicken, brown rice, and salad, they went over the situation, trying to impose some semblance of order to everything they had learned.

But each clue only led to more questions.

"Why do you think my birth mother left me on the church doorstep?" Collette asked. "I mean, I know she was a teen mother, and she probably felt alone and scared. But didn't she have someone she could confide in? What about her parents? Her roommate? Maybe even Nadine."

"Nadine wasn't friends with your mother. I called

my cousin yesterday to ask her about that," Dexter responded. "Rita said that Nadine and Shaylee weren't friends, but Nadine did know her from the neighborhood. Seems Shaylee was shunned for getting pregnant. From what Nadine had heard, after her death, some relatives in Minnesota took the baby."

"Well, obviously they didn't, since I wasn't raised in Minnesota."

"Obviously."

Collette speared a piece of chicken with her fork, more for something to do than because she had a real desire to eat. "Maybe we can find that groundskeeper again. He might've remembered something else."

"It's worth a try," Dexter said.

After they finished dinner, he helped her with the dishes. Collette could barely stifle a yawn a short while later as they sat on the couch. The two glasses of wine she'd had must have relaxed her more than she'd realized, and coupled with the hours she'd spent pouring over the microfiche, it was nearly impossible for her to keep her eyes open.

"I should let you get some rest before we head out," Dexter said. He stood, and Collette walked him to the door. "How's eleven-thirty? As it's New Year's Eve, the reverend should be at the church at the stroke of midnight."

"Eleven-thirty is good."

"I'll meet you back here, then."

"Okay."

Dexter palmed the doorknob, but instead of opening the door, he turned and pulled her into his arms. "Thanks for letting me spoil you tonight."

Before Collette had a chance to respond, Dexter lowered his face to hers and covered her lips in a blood-searing kiss. Her head told her no, don't do this, but her heart said yes, oh yes, please, and Collette could only wrap her arms around Dexter's neck and let him deepen the kiss.

Their tongues twined around one another's, and he rubbed the small of her back as he held her close against him. She could feel his instant arousal, and responded with a quickening of her own. Lord, but she wanted this man.

When Dexter pulled back and looked into her eyes, Collette was lost in his gaze. Looking at her that way he could easily talk her into anything. She was certainly no longer sleepy.

Dexter's warm breath fanned her forehead. "I don't want to go."

Collette didn't say a word. She didn't dare breathe. She couldn't trust what would come out of her mouth.

"Do you want me to go?"

If she said what her heart wanted, that no, she didn't want him to go, what would their relationship be? Would it be anything more than two people who were attracted to each other falling into bed?

Dexter skimmed his lips over her forehead, and Collette's heart fluttered with excitement.

"Dex . . ."

"Tell me you want me to stay," he whispered into her ear. His voice was low and sexy, vibrating through

her entire body. She shut her eyes as the aftershocks
of his voice rocked through her.

"Yes. Stay with me, Dexter."

"Tell me you want me."

"You know I do," she replied, her voice hoarse as
he nibbled her ear.

Dexter pulled back to look at her, as if to see for
himself the truth in her eyes. As he stared at her, she
let her eyes wander over his face, then lower to his
white shirt and black jeans. She could see his arousal,
large and hard, beneath the black fabric.

Brazenly, she reached for him and stroked him,
and felt a surge of power as he moaned.

She stroked him again, feeling him pulsate against
her hand. She ran her hand upward to his firm stomach, where she splayed her fingers, enjoying the feel
of the muscles beneath. She brought her other hand
to his chest, stroking a nipple through his shirt.

And then Dexter was kissing her again, kissing her
while he walked her down the hallway to her bedroom. "Which room?" he asked.

"This one." Collette pointed to her right.

Dexter opened the door, then brought his sweet
lips back down on her mouth as he led her into the
bedroom. They tumbled onto the bed, Collette strad-
dling Dexter.

Slipping his hands beneath her shirt, he pulled it
off her body, then tossed it to the floor. He unclasped
her bra, then took her by the shoulders and eased
her forward, until her breasts hung over his face.
Hungrily, he reached for one, taking the nipple into
his mouth and suckling hard. Collette cried out from

the pleasure of it, then cried out again as he pleasured the other nipple with equal fervor.

The feeling was so wonderful, she thought she would die right there.

When Collette thought she surely couldn't take any more of Dexter's special brand of torture, she pulled back and reached for the snap of his jeans. But Dexter took her wrists in one hand and whirled her over so that she was on her back.

"I've thought about this more times than you know," Dexter told her. "At nights, when I felt lonely, and I wondered why I'd ever let you go . . ."

"I know." She'd thought the same thing more times than she'd like to admit.

Dexter kissed her lips, her neck, her breasts, driving her to the edge of delirium. He paused long enough to disrobe her, disrobe himself, and then slip on a condom before settling between her legs and making them one.

Together, they found their old rhythm. Together, they reached the stars.

Later, Collette lay in the crook of Dexter's arms, the faint sound of his breathing filling the air. She was happy, content. She'd been lying to herself when she said she didn't need this. Being with Dexter again had filled a void in her soul.

There was something about Dexter, a special quality that made her feel completely safe.

If only the here, the now, could last forever. No

tomorrow, no yesterday, just now. Now, was perfect. Now, there were no questions, no doubts.

But tomorrow would come. And what would it hold for them? What did tonight mean to their future?

Collette had tried to fight it, she really had, but her feelings for Dexter had been resurging more and more each day. Now, lying with him like this, much the way they had in the past, she couldn't help but think of the depth of the love they'd once shared. How could a love like that end? And if it had ended once, did Collette want to take another chance only to have it end again? Dealing with heartbreak once had been bad enough; she didn't know if she could handle it again.

Closing her eyes, her naked body pressed to his, she savored the feel of Dexter's strong arm around her waist. She wished they could stay like this all night, but they couldn't. They had to get up and head to the church.

To deal with the ugly truth of what had happened to her mother.

Collette lifted her head. The digital clock beside her bed read ten-thirteen. They had a little time before getting ready. Settling her head back on the pillow, her mind drifted over everything she'd learned in the last week, about her parents' lie, and about her real mother's death. It seemed the only thing she had left were these two arms around her.

Collette sat up. Dexter stirred, but didn't wake. Opening a drawer, she slipped into a nightshirt, then, on a whim, she made her way to her grandmother's bedroom. She lifted the wooden box containing the newspaper articles about Baby Jane.

It was the pictures she wanted to see.

She lifted the first one. Wearing a huge smile, Judy Jenkins held the bundle of joy that had once been her. Victor Jenkins stood with his arms around his wife. They looked like more than proud parents. Their elated expressions said they were eternally grateful for the gift they'd been given, one they hadn't been able to receive naturally.

And strangely, Collette felt a sense of joy. Joy that she'd been the one they'd been so happy to receive. Joy because someone had wanted her, needed her to make their lives complete. They'd given her so much over the years; it was nice to know that she'd been a blessing in their lives.

Collette brushed a tear away and flipped to the next picture. In this one her parents stood with another man and woman. She focused on the couple that stood beside her adoptive parents. The picture had been taken from a distance, making it hard to tell who they were.

Suddenly, something caught her eye.

The feeling that she'd been missing something, that a clue had been staring her in the face for days, finally came full circle. She knew what it was.

The first time she'd seen this photograph, she'd paid scant attention to the cross hanging around the man's neck, but now it seemed to jump out at her like a slap in the face.

A memory of Reverend Evans, clutching his chest

the night he'd fainted and breaking the flat-linked chain around his neck, flashed through her mind.

That chain had borne a heavy, antique silver cross, with a large amethyst in its center, surrounded by four smaller stones on each section. Because it was such an unusual cross, she'd remembered it.

She hadn't made the connection until now.

Her hands shaking, Collette brought the photo closer, moving her focus from the distinctive cross to the man's smiling face.

The smiling face of Reverend Evans.

Fifteen

Clutching the photo, Collette sprinted from her grandmother's bedroom and back to her own room where Dexter lay sleeping.

"Dex." He was already moving, sitting up almost before she called his name. Collette plopped onto the bed beside him and turned on the lamp. "It's him. It's the reverend."

Dexter's eyes went to the picture Collette held. He took it from her hands. As he stared at it, Collette stared at him. "Whoa."

"It's an old photo and he's much younger, but it's definitely him."

"No doubt about it. That slimy . . ."

"Dex, what does it mean?"

"It means we get the truth tonight, even if I have to beat it out of him."

A small smile touched Collette's lips at Dexter's words. It meant the world to know he was helping her fight this battle.

Would he always be there for her? In every way? The question made Collette's heart race and she wondered if that was really what she really wanted.

She enjoyed being with Dexter. Emotionally, she'd come to lean on his support. Sexually, it had felt like coming home. But they were two people leading very different lives today than the ones they had years ago. What if once they reunited it simply wasn't the same?

And that scared her.

She wanted to know what Dexter was feeling, but this wasn't the time to ask. Not when she was an hour away from a showdown with Reverend Evans.

"Collette."

Dexter spoke her name softly, and jerking her head up, she realized she'd been lost in thought.

"Yes, Dex?"

"We should get ready to leave."

"Oh." Disappointment stuck in her throat like a bitter pill. "Of course."

Dexter reached for his briefs from the floor and slipped them on. "I'm gonna shower first." Dexter winked. "Wanna join me?"

No affectionate touch, no term of endearment. The little balloon of hope inside her deflated. But what had Collette expected? For Dexter to profess his undying love for her?

Oh, God, that's exactly what she'd expected. More than that, she'd needed it. Especially after making love.

Now, Collette couldn't help wondering if she'd gotten her hopes up too high—despite her determination not to. Had what they'd just shared been about satisfying lust?

"I don't think showering together is a good idea," Collette said after a moment. "Not right now."

Dexter actually nodded; he didn't protest or try to seduce her into reconsidering. Collette tried to fight the surge of emotions inside her. Tried, but didn't quite succeed.

"All right," Dexter told her. "I'll shower at my place and meet you back here in a little while."

"Sure," Collette said, trying to sound casual.

She knew she'd let her heart cross the line.

Dexter made his way back to his house, wondering why after sharing an incredible experience with Collette, his soul felt deflated.

The sex had been all that he could have wanted and more. It was explosive, like it always had been, and as he'd held her in his arms, Dexter had felt complete.

Opening his front door, Dexter walked into his house. What did he want? After his failed marriage, he'd sworn off relationships. Working at the school and with the kids seemed to give him everything he needed. But now, being with Collette again, he realized that he was missing out on a very wonderful part of life—a mature, satisfying relationship.

He wanted to be with her, yet she was still standoffish. Was there room in her heart for him? He wasn't so sure.

He couldn't put his finger on it, but she seemed distant now. Like she regretted what had happened. And if she regretted it, would they have a chance at a future?

Stop thinking about all this, Dexter told himself. Now

wasn't the time. They needed to deal with the Reverend Evans and close that chapter of Collette's life.

After that, he'd deal with figuring out what the future had in store for them.

There was a chill in the night air.

An omen? Collette wondered.

Another shiver passed through her, and Collette snuggled deeper into her cardigan, but the chill seemed to be coming from inside out.

She was sitting in the passenger seat of Dexter's car. Since they'd left his house ten minutes ago, neither of them had said more than two words to each other. It wasn't like they were fighting, but something was different.

Dexter finally spoke. "I know you're not sure about what's gonna happen, but try not to worry. I'll deal with the reverend."

"Hmm." Collette couldn't think of anything else to say. She wasn't sure if any words would change her mood.

Minutes later, they pulled into the parking lot of the church. It was so full, they had to drive around for a while until they found a spot. When they did, Dexter cut the engine, turned to her and said, "Let's do this."

Collette nodded in agreement. But she missed the touch of his hand across her hand or face like he had done before leaving the car the other occasions they'd come here. And when she got out of the car and met Dexter, she found herself wishing he would wrap a comforting arm around her shoulder.

Instead, he walked briskly to the front door of the church, one purpose on his mind.

It was the same purpose that should be on her mind.

Should be, but wasn't. When had she gotten her priorities so screwed up?

She took a step and stopped when a chill seized her heart.

Seeming to sense her distress, Dexter halted, turned, and walked back toward Collette.

"Hey . . ."

"It's suddenly hitting me." Collette swallowed. "That this is where . . . where my mother died." Her eyes misted with tears. "I didn't think it would affect me like this . . . I never knew her . . . but I can't seem to shake the feeling of how awful it was for her, giving me up, then getting killed."

"I know, sweetheart." He encircled her in his arms.

Closing her eyes, Collette rested her cheek against Dexter's chest. She didn't want to need him, but she couldn't help it.

"I can't have anything else, Dex, but at least I can have closure."

"Ready?" Dexter asked softly.

Pulling back, Collette nodded.

It was now or never.

The church was packed, but the reverend was easy to find. He was standing at the pulpit, preaching.

Collette and Dexter watched him through the glass in the door separating the sanctuary from the narthax.

". . . start the new year with clean hearts and renewed spirits," he was saying when Collette tuned in. "This is the time, brothers and sisters, to recommit yourselves to the . . ." His eyes meeting Collette's, the reverend faltered. He tried to recover so that it wouldn't be noticeable to the congregation. "To the Lord. Can I get an amen?"

"Amen!"

"He's seen us," Collette whispered to Dexter.

"Let's go inside."

"Wait." Collette's eyes scanned the crowd. "There's the groundskeeper!"

"Where?"

Collette pointed to the right. "Third row from the back on the far side."

"You're right. That's him."

The church was filled, but there appeared to be just enough room for Collette to squeeze in beside the grounds keeper. "I'm going in. If I can get to the groundskeeper, I can ask him some questions."

Dexter agreed. "All right."

Quietly, Dexter opened the back door, and Collette slipped into the sanctuary. Some heads turned at their entrance, but eyes didn't linger on them.

"Excuse me." Collette squeezed into the pew where the grounds keeper sat, making space for herself between him and another man. Dexter made his way into the pew behind her.

Glancing to his right, the groundskeeper offered Collette a smile, but shock soon widened his eyes.

Why? she wondered.

The choir began to sing. Realizing this was the best time to talk to him, Collette leaned close to the grounds keeper and said, "Hi. Remember me?"

The grounds keeper looked toward the podium, as if afraid to be seen with her.

"I need to talk to you," Collette continued. "About my mother."

His eyes flashed concern. "I don't want no trouble."

"I'm not here to cause trouble. Just to get answers."

"I can't talk to you," he whispered.

"Why not?"

The groundskeeper didn't respond.

"Please. This is important."

Dexter was leaning forward, his arms resting on Collette's pew. "Maybe we can go into the narthax . . ."

Realizing that Dexter was behind him, the groundskeeper became more agitated. "I don't know nothin'."

"I think you do," Collette said boldly.

"Look," the man answered, sounding nervous. "The reverend . . ."

"Forget the reverend," Dexter said. "He can't hurt you."

"I don't know nothin'. But there's a man, his name is Myron Honeycutt . . ."

"You know Myron?" Collette's heart pounded with hope.

The man's eyes flitted above her head, and Collette whipped around. A familiar looking woman was standing at the end of her pew.

She was the woman Collette had seen with Jabari and that crazy lady two nights ago.

But there was something else.

She was the woman in the picture! The woman standing beside Reverend Evans.

Good Lord, she must be his wife.

Looking down at her sternly, the woman pointed a finger at Dexter and Collette, then motioned for them to come with her.

Collette's heart beat against her ribcage. Glancing over her shoulder, she looked at Dexter to silently ask what they should do.

Dexter leaned forward. He handed her a slip of paper. "Give this to him." With a jerk of the head, he indicated the groundskeeper. Then Dexter stood.

While Dexter diverted the woman's attention, Collette surreptitiously pressed the piece of paper into his palm. "Call us," she whispered.

When she turned, the woman was still waiting, her eyes relaying her displeasure. Clearly, she wasn't going to be happy until Collette was out of the pew as well.

People were starting to look. Collette rose. The woman immediately turned on her heel and led Collette and Dexter to the back doors.

The moment they were out of the sanctuary, she spoke to them. "I want you both to leave."

"We'll leave," Dexter replied. "As soon as we get the answers we came for."

"You'll leave now."

"You know," Dexter began sarcastically, "I just can't understand why a church would keep pushing prospective members away."

"She's his wife, Dexter." At Collette's words, the woman's eyes widened. "Yeah, I know," Collette told her. Then, to Dexter. "She's in the picture with him."

"Look, I don't know what you two want."

"Oh, yes you do," Collette replied. "If it were just the fact that I was left on this doorstep, I might be able to forget about my past and go on with my life. But my mother was murdered. Right behind this church, shortly after she left me here. Someone here knows about her murder, and I'm not leaving until I find out the truth."

"You're crazy."

"If I'm so crazy, why does your husband refuse to talk to me? Why did your son kick us out of the church the other night? And why are you trying to get rid of us now?"

The woman's lips pulled in a tight line.

"What's your name?" Dexter asked.

The woman hesitated, then said, "Gwendolyn. Gwendolyn Evans."

"Mrs. Evans, all we want are some answers," Dexter told her. "Surely, as a minister's wife, you must have some compassion. You've got to understand why this is so important to Collette. And you must understand that your family's refusal to answer simple questions has given us reason to be suspicious."

Gwendolyn swallowed. "What do you want to know?"

"All right. Was Shaylee Simon a member of this church?"

"No."

"But you know she was murdered," Collette said.

Discomfort flashed in the woman's eyes—or was it alarm? "Yes," she replied curtly. "I know."

"I found an article about her death. It said that she was murdered behind this church. Are you saying that that was the first time you'd ever heard of Shaylee Simon?"

"I don't see why that matters."

"It does matter," Collette told her.

"I don't think you'll want to hear what I have to say."

"Why not?" Dexter asked.

Mrs. Evans's eyes went to him. "Because I've always been taught that if you don't have anything nice to say, don't say anything at all."

"So you did know her." When the woman didn't answer, Collette pressed on. "Please, you have to tell me—"

"Look, all I know is that your mother was a tramp who made a lot of enemies. She was a troublemaker. Anyone could have wanted her dead. Are you happy now?"

Anger surged through Collette's body, a protective urge spilling forth from way down in her soul. "Don't you dare speak of my mother that way again."

"You wanted the truth."

"She was a good person. She left me here, at this church, a good place, because she loved me."

"If that's what you want to believe." Mrs. Evans's voice dripped with bitterness.

"She's been dead for twenty-seven years. Why are you so angry? So hateful?"

"This conversation is over."

Mrs. Evans whirled on her heel, turning for the sanctuary door. Before she could escape, Collette grabbed her by the arm.

"Let go of me, you dirty slut."

Stunned at the woman's awful words, Collette dropped her arm. As quickly as she did, Mrs. Evans regained her composure. Then, opening the door, she disappeared.

"Did you see that?" Collette asked Dexter. "Did you hear her?"

"Doesn't sound so Christian-like, does it?"

"She sounds . . ." Collette shook her head. "She sounds evil."

"I'm not sure this is going to work," Dexter said after a moment. "Maybe it's time we try something drastic. Like going to the media, or something to make them sweat."

Collette glanced through the window into the church sanctuary. From the front row, the old lady who'd hissed those awful words to her had her head turned and was glaring at her.

Her eyes darted to the left. Jabari, on the other side of the aisle, also looked back at them as his mother took her place beside him.

Finally, Collette's eyes went to the pulpit. As Reverand Evans spoke about the wonder of God's word, his eyes met Collette's, but he couldn't hold her gaze and looked away.

Hypocrite, she thought.

And then a bitter thought hit her. Her stomach churning, she turned to Dexter.

"Her killer is in this room."

Dexter's eyebrows shot up. "You think so?"

Collette nodded grimly. "I know it, Dex. I feel it." Her eyes scanned the room again, and the sick feeling in her stomach worsened.

She knew she was right.

Now, she had to find a way to prove it.

The darkness of the night shrouded them.

"What did you tell them?"

"Nothin'," the groundskeeper replied. It was cold, and he shivered. He didn't understand what the big deal was anyway, why they didn't want him to speak to the woman and her friend.

An arm tightened around his wrist. "You must have said something. Think, Eddie. I told you, they're out to destroy us. To destroy this church."

Eddie didn't understand how that could happen, but he was a simple man. Maybe he didn't know. "I told 'em to talk to Myron. That maybe he could help 'em."

"Damn. They'll contact him. What else?"

Seeing as how they were outside the church, Eddie didn't want to lie. Lying was a sin. "Well, she gave me her number. Said for me to call if I could help."

"Where is it?"

Eddie dug it out of his pocket.

"Thank you, Eddie. Don't you worry about calling her. I'll take care of that."

"You will?"

"Yep. I'll do whatever I can to help her, okay? So don't you lose a moment's sleep over it."

And I'll take care of her, just like I took care of her mother.

Sixteen

As Dexter brought his car to a full stop in his drive-way, he turned and glanced at Collette. She hadn't spoken a word to him since leaving the church. She'd sat in his car, her arms folded across her chest like she was miffed.

Horns blared as cars drove by and Dexter glanced at the digital clock. "Collette."

She didn't face him. "What?"

"It's Midnight." He paused. "Happy New Year."

She met and held his eyes in the dimly lit car. "Happy New Year," she said softly, but her voice was so dispirited, her heart obviously wasn't in it.

Dexter leaned across the seat and planted a gentle kiss on her temple. Collette didn't respond.

"Hey," Dexter began.

"I have to go," she abruptly said. She reached for the door handle.

"Collette." Dexter spoke firmly, and she stopped before opening the door. But she didn't look at him. "Collette, what's wrong?"

"You know what's wrong."

"No, not really."

Huffing, Collette faced him. "I don't appreciate you dragging me out of the church before I had a chance to talk to the reverend."

So that was it. Once Collette had shared her thought that her mother's killer was in the room, she'd wanted to go back into the sanctuary and confront the reverend. It was anger talking, for surely confronting him in front of a church full of people didn't make sense.

"Tonight wasn't the right time."

"Really? When would be a good time for you, Dexter?" She was back to calling him by his full name.

"It's not about what's good for me. It's about what's the best thing to do. Maybe we should get the police involved."

"Like they're going to do anything."

Dexter frowned as he stared at Collette. "Why are you so pessimistic?"

"If the police didn't have enough evidence to arrest anyone back then, what are they gonna do now?"

Dexter considered her words. "Maybe it doesn't seem like a lot, but what little we've learned might help them."

"Yeah, right."

He placed a hand on her shoulder. "I'm not sure what else we can do."

That's what had her so frustrated, knowing that this was beyond her control. "I just feel like I should be doing something else. Tracking down more leads. *Something.*"

"You've done a helluva lot already, considering you're not Agatha Christie."

She frowned at him. "I'm trying to be serious, Dexter."

"I'm sorry." Then, "What do you suggest?"

"I guess at this point I'll try to find Myron Honeycutt."

"Okay. We can do that tomorrow."

"No, I'll do it. I don't need your help, Dexter."

At Collette's words, Dexter stilled. He could only stare at her, dumbfounded.

Collette pushed the door open and stepped out of the car.

As Dexter opened his door, Collette was charging across his front lawn to her house. He sprinted after her and reached her before she could open the door.

"Hey," he said. "Why are you acting like this? Pushing me away?"

"This is my problem. I'll handle it my way."

"Now you don't need my help, is that it?"

Ignoring him, Collette pushed the key into the lock and opened the door. Determined not to back down, he followed her inside.

"Dexter, I really don't have time for this now. I just want to be alone."

"Why?"

"Because I can't take the pressure anymore."

"I'm not pressuring you."

"Yes, you are. I told you I didn't want to get involved with you, at least not until I closed this chapter of my life with my mother. But somehow we ended up in bed tonight."

"We *both* wanted that."

"Yeah, well . . . you got what you wanted."

Collette turned and strolled toward the kitchen, but Dexter was hot on her trail. "What the hell does that mean?"

She didn't face him. "I don't know."

"You must know. You said it."

Slowly, exhaling a sigh, Collette turned. "What do you want, Dexter?"

"With us, you mean?"

"Yes."

He lifted his shoulders in a shrug. "I want to keep seeing you."

"Why?"

"Because I'm attracted to you."

"Hmm." She turned around again.

Gripping her shoulders, Dexter made her face him. "What do you want, Collette?"

"I want to know what happened to my mother. I don't want to be confused about my feelings for you. But right now, being around you is confusing everything. I can't concentrate on my mother, and that's what I need to do right now."

"Fine, I understand that, but we're friends . . ."

"Friends." Collette's gaze dropped to the ground. "Aren't we?"

Collette couldn't meet his eyes. *Friends*. As if their lovemaking had been a casual fling to him. "I don't make love to my friends, Dexter."

"Is that what this is about?" When she didn't answer, Dexter placed a finger beneath her chin and forced her to meet his eyes.

"I know, guys don't know what the big deal is about sex, right?"

"And that's how you think I am? Just like most other guys?"

"Maybe."

Before she knew what was happening, he gripped her by her upper arms and pulled her to him. Her body hit his with an *ooompf*, and she was all too aware that her heart was beating overtime being near him. The worst part was, she wanted to be near him. She liked how it felt to have her breasts crushed to his chest, his strong hands wrapped around her arms.

"I don't know how you can say that, Collette. I've let you know how much I wanted you from the moment I saw you again."

"That's part of the problem. You keep saying you won't rush me . . ."

"Make up your mind, Collette. You can't be upset that I'm rushing you in one breath, then peeved that I'm not running down the aisle with you in the next."

He was right. She was being wishy-washy. She didn't know herself or what she wanted.

But she did know that being this close to Dexter right now was not going to help her think clearly. She struggled against him, and he released her.

"All right," she said softly. "You want to know what I'm feeling? I'm having a very tough time right now with all that life means, how uncertain it is. How it sucks sometimes."

"I hear you, Collette. I never thought I'd lose my father when I did. I never thought I'd get divorced once I got married. I know you didn't expect to receive that letter from your grandmother, that it turned your life upside down. I know it's tough to deal with, but that's the way life is sometimes. It throws tough stuff at you, and it doesn't give you any guarantees."

As Collette gazed into his eyes, sadness filled her own. "What about us, Dexter?"

He shrugged. "I know I want you, that I want to work things out."

"But you can't guarantee that they will."

"No one can guarantee anything."

Her heart feeling like it was tearing in two, Collette stepped away from him. This was exactly what she'd feared, getting herself caught up in her old feelings for Dexter, only to have him hurt her again.

Maybe he was right. Maybe life offered no guarantees.

But that wasn't what she wanted to hear.

And she certainly didn't have to offer up her heart if there was no promise he wouldn't hurt her.

"You need to go now, Dexter."

"Collette . . ."

"No. Go. And I think it's time I learned to stand on my own two feet, so as I said, I'm going to find Myron and question him."

"I don't think . . ."

"This isn't about what you think."

Collette's words were like a knife in his heart.

She was pushing him out of her life, and this time he had no choice but to go.

He knew she wanted a guarantee, not promises. But how could he give that to her when life offered none?

Turning, Dexter lumbered toward the door. When he reached it, he stopped and faced her.

"Just go."

So he did.

The night had lasted forever.

Collette had hardly slept, tossing and turning, her mind filled with a million thoughts. Now that it was morning, she didn't feel like getting out of bed.

She had done the right thing, hadn't she? He had flat-out told her he couldn't offer her any guarantees, so why should she give him her heart again?

Life may offer no guarantees, but she could control some things, and keeping hold of her heart was one of them.

Still, she felt the urge to get up and call him, or to go over to his house and see him one more time.

But she couldn't.

Not after she'd told him to stay away. She'd left no room for negotiation, so now, even if it killed her, she had to stay away from him.

Restless, Collette stood and walked to the bedroom window. Outside, the cloudless morning sky was a perfect cerulean blue. It was the first day of the new year but it did not bring hope.

It had been less than twelve hours since she'd ended all talk of a future relationship with Dexter. It was the best thing to do, she told herself. But for someone who had been uncompromising about her decision when she'd made it, she certainly was having her doubts now.

She missed his low, seductive voice. She missed his calm, rational advice. She missed him, period.

Maybe she should go over and ask for his help finding Myron. But if she were to do that, she would look worse than a fool; she'd look schizophrenic.

No, she'd made her bed. Now she had to lie in it.

Dexter needed to think, so he grabbed his basketball, went to his school, and shot hoops.

Thoughts bounced around in his head like the ball bouncing as he dribbled.

While he told himself he'd done the best he could yesterday and had answered Collette's questions as honestly as possible, he couldn't help but feel a measure of guilt.

He stopped, jumped, and took a shot. It hit the rim of the basket and bounced away. He ran to retrieve it, but he couldn't as easily outrun the memory of sadness in Collette's eyes last night when he'd told her there were no guarantees.

That was the truth, wasn't it? Bad things happened all the time, plans went awry.

Dexter took another shot, and this time the ball went in the basket. But there was no joy in it, not while he had a gaping hole in his heart.

The nearest phone was at a gas station a couple of miles away, but Collette walked the distance anyway. There was no way she would ask to use Dexter's phone.

Besides, the walk had helped clear her mind and focus once again on the task of solving her mother's murder.

There were a few M. Honeycutts in the white pages, and one Myron. She jotted down all the numbers, then slipped change into the payphone to make the first call.

The number that belonged to Myron simply rang and rang. She called the three others and learned that they weren't the right ones.

Once again, she dialed Myron's number. Once again, it simply rang.

It was a couple of hours later when Dexter returned home. His body was soaked with perspiration from his rigorous workout, and the first thing he wanted to do was take a shower.

Hoping that Collette had tried to reach him, he checked his answering machine.

The sound of an older man's voice filled the air. "Hello." It sounded tentative. "My name is Myron Honeycutt, and I'm looking for Collette."

Myron Honeycutt! Dexter's heart accelerated.

"I understand she's looking for me, and I want to talk now. Tell you what I know. It's been too long." Pause. "I'll be in the alley of the church after sunset. You know the one. Please meet me there."

Dexter rewound the tape to listen to it again. Then, he hurried to Collette's house to tell her who had called.

He didn't find her there. After banging on the

door for several minutes, it was apparent that she wasn't home.

Maybe it was better that she wasn't home. If he told her about Myron's call, she'd no doubt want to meet the man by herself.

He wasn't about to let her do that.

No, he'd meet the man. He'd hear what he had to say.

Seventeen

Don't panic, Collette told herself, when she opened her door that evening and found Jabari Evans standing on her doorstep. Though it was hard to heed her own advice when fear was making her heart pound so furiously that she was sure he could hear it. *Just act cool.*

"Jabari. To what do I owe this honor?"

"May I come in?"

He was polite, demure, very unlike the bully he'd been at the church a few days ago. "Why?"

"Because you're right. There're some things about your mother we haven't told you. It's time you learned the truth."

"You know what happened to her?"

"Yes. And I want to tell you about it. Will you let me come in?"

Collette's pulse quickened. She was excited to hear that Jabari was ready to come clean about what he knew, but she was also afraid. Should she let him in?

Yesterday, she'd thought she was tough enough to deal with a situation like this on her own. Now, she desperately wished for Dexter to be here. Taking a quick glance to her left, she saw that his car was gone.

"Please," Jabari added.

Jabari's car was in her driveway, she noted. If Dexter came home, he'd realize she had company and come over to check on her.

"All right," Collette finally said. She stepped backward, allowing him to enter her home. Her purse was on the sofa. She'd sit next to it. Inside it was a can of mace—just in case.

Jabari entered the house and closed the door. Collette made her way to the sofa. She sat beside her purse. Surreptitiously, she unzipped the zipper, preparing for easy access should that become necessary.

Jabari sat in her father's old recliner.

"What do you know?" she asked him.

Jabari inhaled, exhaled, then began speaking. "Your mother was murdered."

"That much I know, Jabari."

"I figured as much. But I know who killed her."

Oh, God, she thought. "Who?"

"There's a guy who used to come by the church sometimes. He was a drifter, and sometimes my father would help him out by giving him odd jobs."

"Myron Honeycutt."

"You know of him?"

"I saw an article that said he'd been questioned in regards to my mother's murder, but released."

"Yes, but I believe he was responsible for her death."

"Do you have any proof of that?"

Jabari slowly nodded. "That night—the night you

were left on the church doorstep—I saw your mother.
I found her body."

"Oh my God. But the article, it said Myron Honeycutt had found her."

"He was there, that's for sure. Anyway, there was a
church social going on that night and I stepped outside for some air. I thought I heard something in the
alley behind the church, some screams. So I ran toward the alley. But when I got there I didn't see anything.

"Then, I saw someone's leg protruding from behind a garbage can. I went closer . . . and I saw that
it was your mother."

A moan escaped Collette's throat.

"The next thing I knew, my father was running
into the alley. He saw me with the body."

"But if you knew it was Myron Honeycutt, why
didn't you say so? Why did the article say he had
found her?"

"My father wanted to protect me. You see, I was
only sixteen. He didn't want me to have to deal with
all sorts of police questioning. So when he got to the
scene, he told me to go back into the church and
pretend I hadn't seen a thing. It was hard, but I did
it."

"But why did my mother go to your church? You
were about her age. Do you know who she was seeing . . . who the father of her baby was?"

Glancing away, Jabari shook his head.

"You say you saw Myron Honeycutt. Where did he
come from?"

"Just after I found the body, I saw something in

the shadows and called out. He stepped into the light, and I saw him. Then my father showed up and sent me away."

"So you didn't see him kill her."

"No, but he was the only one there right after I heard your mother crying out."

Collette frowned. Was Myron Honeycutt her mother's killer? And if he was, why hadn't the police arrested him?

A knock on the door interrupted her thoughts.

Dexter.

Jumping from the sofa, Collette practically flew to the door. But when she opened it, she didn't see Dexter. Instead, Reverend Evans stood outside.

Whirling around, she saw that Jabari was on his feet and approaching her. Her heart leaped into her throat.

The reverend rushed into the house, stepping between her and Jabari.

"What are you doing here, Dad? I told you I would take care of this."

Take care of this?

"I know," the reverend said, his breath coming in gasps as if he'd been running. "I saw your note. But I can't let you do this, son. I can't let you kill her."

Imani, the seventh principle of Kwanzaa.

Dexter tried to focus on that as he waited in the dark alley at the back of the church. Faith had led him to this spot, and he knew that tonight he'd learn the truth.

He wanted that so much. Wanted it for Collette, to give her the closure she needed, and perhaps restore her faith in happiness.

He'd told her that life had no guarantees, but he'd forgotten about faith. Faith could see you through anything.

He wished this was all a bad dream, that he could be at home with his family celebrating the last night of Kwanzaa. But this situation was real, and he would see this through.

For Collette.

Hearing a sound, Dexter turned his head to the left. A dark form appeared out of the shadows.

"Myron?" he called. "Myron Honeycutt?"

Jabari's eyes narrowed in a quizzical gaze. "What are you talking about, Dad?"

"There's been enough blood," the reverend said in a sad voice. "It has to end, and it has to end now."

As Reverend Evans had walked into the house to approach his son, Collette was close to the door. *Run!* her mind screamed.

She whirled around and darted for the door.

Two strong hands wrapped around her arm, stopping her.

She turned to see the reverend. "Please," she begged. "Please let me go." *Oh, Dexter. Where are you?*

"No," the reverend said calmly. As though this were a casual friendly visit, he sauntered to the door . while still holding her arm and closed it. He turned the lock. "Not yet."

Collette's eyes frantically darted between the reverend and his son. She'd been set up! Jabari had come to her, pretending to have answers. Now his father was here so they could both kill her, the way they had killed her mother.

And no one would be the wiser.

Collette squirmed, trying to free her arm, but the older man who looked like he'd once played football was too strong for her.

"I'm not going to hurt you," the reverend said.

There was something about the way he looked at her, something oddly comforting; she stopped fighting.

"What do you want?" she asked.

A grim expression set on the reverend's face. "To tell you the truth. Finally." He turned to Jabari. "I'm sorry, son. I have to do this."

"Dad . . ."

"No." The reverend cut him off. "Sit down, Jabari. And Collette, if you'd sit too."

There was nothing she could do. She was stuck here with the two of them, with no phone, and no sign of Dexter. But at least she was able to return to her purse with her can of mace.

Sitting, she folded her arms over her lap so she could reach into the purse without anyone noticing. Her fingers curled around what she sought.

"What happened that night?" she asked.

The reverend sat on the sofa with her, leaving some space between them. "Your mother came to the church that night. She came to talk to me."

"You were her minister?"

Reverend Evans's Adam's apple rose and fell as he swallowed. "She trusted me, yes. And I failed her."

"Reverend, you're talking in riddles. If you really want to tell me the truth, just tell me."

"All right." The reverend nodded. "Your mother came to the church to see me . . . about the baby."

"Why? Were you the one helping set up the adoption?"

"I was—"

"Dad," Jabari said, interrupting him.

"Stop it, Jabari. If I'd come clean then, I could have stopped all this madness. I could have stopped you from killing Shaylee."

Jabari's eyes nearly popped out of his head. "What? You think *I* killed her?"

"I saw you, Jabari. I saw you with her limp body in your arms when I went into the alley."

"I didn't kill her, Dad. I told you that that night."

"He had a rough start as a child," Reverend Evans said to Collette, as though that would excuse his son murdering a woman. "As a baby, he had to have heart surgery. He almost died, but he fought to survive. Such a little thing, yet he had so much zest for life . . . After that, we changed his name to Jabari, which means brave in Swahili. They say kids don't remember, but I think he did, and it affected him . . ."

"Dad, will you stop the rambling?"

The reverend shot a look at his son. "I'm trying to say . . . I take full responsibility for your actions, Jabari. You were merely a child, afraid that your family would be torn apart . . ."

"Dad, I swear, I *didn't* kill her! I could never kill anyone."

Emitting a frustrated cry, Collette slapped a hand to her forehead. "What is going on?"

"I failed," the reverend answered. "As a man, as a father, as a man of God." He paused. "But I just couldn't turn in my son."

Jabari shot to his feet. "Is this what you've believed all these years? That I killed Shaylee?"

Collette watched father and son. Something about the way Jabari had spoken finally got through to the reverend.

"Are you saying . . . ?"

"I'm saying I didn't kill her." Jabari looked to Collette. "Like I told you, I think it was Myron Honeycutt."

"You were serious about that story?" Pain flashed over Reverend Evans's face, his eyes taking on a faraway look. "All this time, I thought you were trying to cover up what you did."

"Why would Jabari want to kill my mother?" Collette suddenly asked. Something didn't make sense.

"I thought it was because he was afraid he would lose me . . . to her."

Ice cold reality slammed Collette like a sledgehammer to the stomach. "Oh my God. Are you saying . . ."

Reverend Evans met her eyes, tears welling in his own. "Yes, that's exactly what I'm saying. Collette, I'm your father."

Eighteen

"Myron Honeycutt?"

The dark form moved closer: one step, two, three, until it was finally under the dim glow of a lightbulb. That's when Dexter saw that it was *not* Myron Honeycutt. It couldn't be, because it was a woman.

Gwendolyn Evans.

"Mrs. Evans?" What was she doing here? Had Myron been in touch with her, too?

"Hello."

Dexter strained to see behind her. Was Myron there, hiding in the shadows, afraid even after all this time?

"Where's Myron?" he asked.

Gwendolyn walked slowly, purposefully, toward him. "Myron couldn't make it."

"So he asked you to come instead?"

"Something like that."

She had an odd, emotionless expression on her face. Something about it didn't sit well with Dexter.

"Where's Collette?" she asked.

"She couldn't make it either," Dexter replied, being as evasive as Gwendolyn had been.

"Myron asked *her* to come." Her voice had an icy quality that made the hairs on the back of Dexter's neck stand on end.

"Well, all things considered—there is a murderer on the loose—I didn't think she should come alone."

"So she's here?" Gwendolyn arched an eyebrow.

"Why did Myron send you here, Mrs. Evans? What did he want you to tell Collette?"

Glancing at the ground, she muttered something unintelligible.

"Excuse me?"

Her head whipped up, her eyes wide. "Collette was supposed to be here—not you." Dexter watched as she ran a hand over her short hair. "You've ruined everything."

A wave of icy cold fear slithered down his spine. *This woman's crazy,* he realized.

He took a step backward. "All right. Why don't you tell Myron to call Collette and set up another time?"

"I'm afraid he can't do that."

"Why not?"

"Because he's dead." There was movement, then the light caught the object that appeared in her hand. A gun. "And you're going to have to die, too."

Collette's mouth nearly hit the floor as she stared at the reverend. "My father? *You're* my father?"

Not meeting her eyes, Reverend Evans nodded.

Collette shot to her feet. "No. *No!*"

"I know this is the last thing you want to hear. But it's true, and I've lied long enough."

Collette's entire body shook with shock and disbelief. How could this be true? "You're a reverend. You were *married!* How could you?"

"I loved your mother."

Collette threw her hands over her ears. "No. Stop lying." Yet it was the first thing he'd said that didn't sound like a lie, the first thing that made sense, even if being related to the reverend was too hard to accept.

I'm your father.

"I did love your mother," the reverend continued. "Even though I knew it was wrong. I was married, I was twice her age. I was weak. A disgrace to the ministry. That's why I had to end it.

"When she told me she was pregnant, I didn't know what to do. I went to my wife, told her the truth. She was livid. And, I suppose, jealous of Shaylee. You see, after Jabari, she couldn't have any more children.

"She told me to make sure Shaylee didn't say a thing, that we'd help find the baby a good home. I agreed, because I didn't know what else to do. Jabari had heard his mother and me fighting about Shaylee, and he was scared he was going to lose me. I . . . I couldn't abandon my family, no matter how much I loved Shaylee. Our love was forbidden. No one would have let us live in peace.

"My mother-in-law . . ." Reverend Evans shook his head sorrowfully. "She was especially disappointed in me. She's always been a devout Christian, but she forgave me, certain I'd been seduced by the devil. I never believed that—it was my fault. Your mother was only a child, after all—but given all the adversity I was facing and what she would face too, I felt it was best to push her away. But I promised Shaylee I'd help her financially. It was the least I could do.

"But that didn't satisfy Shaylee. She had nobody. Her mother had died a couple years before. She'd never known her father. She was alone, and she was scared. She didn't want to raise the baby by herself. I suggested adoption, but she said no."

"Then why did she leave me on a church doorstep? If she didn't want to give me up for adoption, why would she do that?"

"I think she wanted to force me to take action, to take responsibility for the baby. In fact, the same night she left you at my church, we'd spoken; she told me how much she wanted to give the baby a name. She didn't want her child—you—to grow up with the stigma of not having a father. I told her I couldn't discuss that with her at the time, but I'd talk to her the next week. She agreed, but I sensed she wasn't happy, that maybe she'd do something drastic. There was a church social going on, and through the window, I glimpsed her hanging around outside. So, a short while later, I went outside to find her. That's when I saw Jabari standing over her body in the alley . . ."

The reverend was telling a crazy tale, one that had both Jabari and Collette captivated, and as much as Collette wanted to dismiss it, she knew that it was entirely true. And surprisingly, she felt a measure of empathy for him. She could see the agony and guilt in his eyes as he retold the story. He was a man of

God who'd taken a wrong turn, and was still living with the guilt of his mistake years later.

"But if you didn't claim me as your daughter, who signed my adoption papers given the fact that my mother was dead?"

"I had someone forge your mother's signature. It was predated before her death. I had arranged for a private adoption with the Jenkins. I knew your adoptive parents. They were members of my church and had wanted a child for years. This seemed the perfect solution."

It was all too wild and bizarre to digest. But the pieces of the puzzle were finally fitting together. One question remained. If neither Reverend Evans nor Jabari had killed her mother, then who had?

"Who killed my mother?" she asked.

The reverend contemplated the question, then shrugged. "If it wasn't Jabari, then I don't know."

"What about Myron?"

"No," Reverend Evans said. "Myron kept promising me he wouldn't tell anyone what he saw. He felt I'd done a lot to help him by giving him odd jobs and such, so he felt a certain loyalty to me. That's why I thought he was referring to you, Jabari." His forehead creased as he stared at his son. "But if it wasn't you . . ."

Gwendolyn Evans.

The name sounded in Collette's brain as if someone had actually whispered it.

Maybe, just maybe, someone had.

"Your wife," Collette said anxiously. "Who else could it be? You said she was angry, jealous . . ."

Reverend Evans was a light-complectioned man, but his skin grew paler when Collette mentioned his wife. "Oh, dear God in heaven." He closed his eyes and gritted his teeth, as though in pain. "That night . . . I wondered where she was. She said she wasn't feeling well and had been in the bathroom . . ."

"I have to tell Dexter." Collette ran to the door. She needed to use his phone as well—to call the police.

Collette banged and banged on Dexter's door but got no response. Of course, she realized belatedly, he wasn't home. His car still wasn't here.

The reverend and his son were behind her, but they said nothing. They had to know she was going to call the police, yet neither was trying to stop her.

Collette needed to get inside. She had to use the phone. She tried the door. It didn't open. Frustrated, she slapped a palm on the door.

That's when she saw the piece of paper taped to the door. She quickly unfolded it.

Collette, if you get this, don't be upset. Myron Honey-cutt called and left a message for you to meet him at the church. I've gone in your place. I'll come by later to tell you everything.

"The church," Collette said, hurriedly. "He said Myron called and asked to meet him at the church."

"Myron?" Reverend Evans asked, sounding skeptical. "The last time I visited him, he was legally blind."

"It's not him." Collette's voice was a horrified whisper as she realized the truth. "We have to go. Now!"

"My car," Jabari said, running toward the white Intrepid pulled up in front of Collette's house.

Collette and Reverend Evans scrambled after Jabari. They all piled into the car, then sped off into the night.

Dexter's mind raced with his options of how he could best handle this situation: he could turn and run, but Gwendolyn might shoot him in the back; he could try to convince her that this was the wrong thing to do, or he could try to disarm her.

"No one has to die," Dexter said calmly.

"If you had just left it alone. But you couldn't, and you must be punished. Shaylee was a little whore who wanted to steal my husband. But I couldn't let her do that. I couldn't let her destroy my family. They were all I had. My whole world."

Gwendolyn had killed Shaylee. She'd killed Myron. There was already blood on her hands; what was to stop her from killing him?

"I understand." Dexter had counseled many troubled teens. Maybe he could use the same techniques to get through to Gwendolyn. "Who wouldn't? You felt threatened."

"Yes."

"Angry, probably."

"Yes."

"And those are perfectly natural feelings. We all have them. But think about what you're doing right now. It's only going to make things worse." When Gwendolyn didn't respond, Dexter continued, hoping he was getting through to her. "I know you didn't want to hurt anyone. You felt threatened, and it happened. But you don't have to make that same mistake again . . ."

He was getting through to her. She was lowering the gun.

Dexter lunged forward . . .

A single gunshot pierced the night air as Jabari pulled the car into the church parking lot.

"Oh my God," Collette said, silently praying she wasn't too late.

"That came from the alley," Reverend Evans said.

Collette threw her door open and jumped out of the car. *Please, God. Don't let Dexter be hurt,* she prayed as she ran. *Don't let me be too late.*

Jabari and his father—her father—were in hot pursuit as she rounded the corner to the alley. Dexter and Gwendolyn's bodies were practically entwined, and she realized that they were both fighting for control of the gun.

"Gwendolyn!" Reverend Evans's deep voice boomed in the alley.

It was enough to distract his wife, and as she threw a startled glance their way, Dexter forced the gun from her hand. He raised it to Mrs. Evans.

"No!" the reverend cried.

"You're going to jail," Dexter said to Mrs. Evans. He had no intention of shooting her, but held the gun steady on her to make sure she didn't try to get away.

Reverand Evans ran up and grabbed his wife in his arms as she broke down and sobbed.

Collette ran toward Dexter, throwing her arms around his neck. "Oh, Dexter." She molded her body to his, relieved to once again feel it against hers. What if they hadn't arrived when they did? What if Gwendolyn had shot him?

What if she'd been too late?

"She killed my mother," Collette said, pulling back to look into Dexter's face.

"I know, sweetheart." He ran a hand over her hair.

"And the reverend . . . he's my . . . he's my father."

Dexter shot a glance over Collette's head in the direction of the reverend, who was holding his wife as she bawled. The man met and held his gaze, a contrite look passing in his eyes.

Yes, it all did come back to the reverend. But could Collette handle this news?

Dexter knew that he'd be there for her, that he'd see her through that, just as he'd seen her through this.

Dexter looked down at Collette, then at the gun in his right hand.

"We have to call the police," Dexter announced.

"I know," the reverend responded. Tears brimmed in his eyes. "All right. Let's go in the church. We can call from there."

* * *

Later, after the police had arrested Mrs. Evans, Collette and Dexter returned to her place. Reverend Evans and Jabari hadn't said much to her as they'd been busy consoling the agitated Mrs. Evans. It was just as well. Collette wasn't quite ready to come to terms with the fact that the reverend was her father.

Her eyes went to the portrait of her parents that hung on the wall. No, Joseph Evans wasn't her father. Victor Jenkins was her father. Just as Judy Jenkins was her mother. They were her parents, always would be, and no one could take that away from her.

But there would always be a special place in her heart for the mother she'd never known, the mother whom she knew without a doubt had loved her.

Now, sitting on her sofa, she felt a mixture of the many different emotions brought on by the past week's events: fear, anxiety, melancholy, sadness.

But there was also happiness. Happiness like she hadn't felt in a long time.

Even though Dexter was the one who'd come close to losing his life tonight, he was the one taking care of her. He wouldn't take no for an answer.

The man was stubborn. Perhaps too stubborn for his own good. But, she realized, a smile touching her lips as she stretched out on the sofa, she liked his brand of stubbornness.

Collette listened to Dexter in the kitchen. Cupboards opened, the kettle whistled. And all the while, she found herself thinking that she was the luckiest woman in the world to have him in her life.

But to what extent would he be in her life? As a friend, a lover, or future husband?

"Here."

Surprised to see Dexter standing before her, Collette quickly sat up and accepted the mug of tea he offered. "Thanks."

"It's chamomile."

He was strong, yet sensitive. Gorgeous. Thoughtful. God, he really was the entire package.

He sat beside her. "You okay?"

"Yeah," she replied. "It's been a roller coaster ride, but it's finally over now."

"And how do you feel?"

"Strangely, I feel relieved. I feel awful for what happened to my mother, but I never knew her. As for the reverend, I don't know how I feel about him. I do think he's sorry for everything and that he'll live with the guilt for the rest of his life. And you know what else? I feel a sense of peace. My mother loved me, Dexter. She didn't want to give me up. She loved me, and that means the world to me."

"It's the seventh night of Kwanzaa."

"I know. I was thinking about that. About the principle of faith. You encouraged me to have faith. I didn't get the answers I necessarily wanted, but I got closure, and peace."

"And now?"

Glancing away, Collette stared into her tea. Now what? Why was she afraid to speak what was in her heart? That she wanted Dexter in her life for as long as she could have him, even though life gave no guarantees.

She loved him. She'd never stopped.

Dexter stood. "I'd better go."

She didn't respond at first, merely watched him as he slowly walked toward the door. When he finally reached the door, she stood. "Wait."

He turned and faced her with a hopeful look.

"Don't go."

He gave her a tentative look. "Collette?"

Go for it. "I can't thank you enough, Dex. For standing by me through all this."

"I told you I would."

"I know. And you kept your word, even though I took you away from celebrating Kwanzaa."

"There's next year," he said. A small smile lifted his lips. "And who knows? Maybe you'll be back to celebrate it with me."

"Maybe."

They were skirting around the issue. She could feel he was holding back as much as she was.

"You think you'll be back next year?"

"You want me back?"

"What if I said I didn't want you to leave?"

At his words, Collette's heart beat a rapid staccato in her chest. And she couldn't think of a thing to say.

"You know how much I want you, don't you?"

Collette's mouth opened, but she couldn't form any words.

Dexter stepped toward her. "Yesterday, you asked me if I could give you a guarantee about our future, if we were to get together. I told you I couldn't." He paused. "Well, I didn't quite mean that."

"No?"

Dexter shook his head. "No. What I should have said was that while life has no guarantees, there's one thing I *can* guarantee you." Dexter reached for her face, tenderly stroked it. "As long as I live, I'll do whatever I can to make you happy. Because I always want to see you smiling." He trailed a finger over her mouth. "Sweetie, you have no idea what that beautiful smile of yours does to me."

Collette's breath caught in her throat. "Dex . . ."

"I love you," he said. "It's as simple and as complicated as that. And I want to spend the rest of my life loving you."

A hot tear fell onto Collette's cheek. "Oh, Dex."

"I don't know if that's enough for you, Collette, but I'm praying it will be."

"I couldn't ask for more." And that was true. Dexter had been there through this whole ordeal, had been patient and caring and understanding—with no expectations. Would she ever find a better man? She doubted it. She certainly had never come close to feeling for anyone else what she felt for him.

"I don't want to spend my life thinking about the things that can keep us apart. I don't want to spend my life regretting the past. I lost my birth mother before I ever got to know her. I couldn't control that. But I can control what I do now. And what I want is to spend my life loving you."

"Oh, baby." Dexter drew her into his arms. Immediately, she rested her head on his shoulder, finally feeling whole, and at peace, safe in the arms of the man she loved. To her surprise, she found herself letting out all the emotions she'd kept buried. She cried. For herself. For her mother. For almost pushing Dexter away.

Dexter's hands framed her face. With his thumbs, he gently brushed away her tears. Then slowly, like a man with patience, he edged her closer. But his eyes said he wanted her with a passion and unity of oneness neither of them had yet experienced.

His lips finally covered hers, and her eyes fluttered shut. His kisses were hot and sweet, hungry and skillful. They'd made love yesterday, but that suddenly seemed so long ago.

Too long.

Wrapping her arms around his neck, she moved closer and flattened her breasts against his hard chest. And the kiss accelerated, became more passionate, until both were lost in a whirlwind of desire they couldn't escape.

Dexter guided her to the bedroom and to the bed. He slipped on a condom, then, lying back, he pulled her onto him, never taking his lips from hers.

And as they finally found their way back to each other, their bodies and souls uniting as one, Collette knew that she and Dexter had made their way home.

Two hearts. One beat. One love.

Home is where the heart is.

And they were home to stay.

Epilogue

One year later

"*Habari gani?*" Standing at the head of the table, Dexter addressed the large group at the dining-room table.

"*Imani!*" everyone answered at once.

Imani. Faith.

It was exactly one year after that night at the church when Collette had learned the answers to the questions of her past. Faith had gotten her through the ordeal. And faith had rewarded her with a much richer life and sense of who she was.

After her story had made the news, Shaylee's roommate had come forward. Through Alison Ball, Collette had gotten to know her mother. She felt a very special closeness to the birth mother she'd never known—a bond—because she was getting to know her through the woman who'd been her best friend.

Shaylee Simon had also been an artist. She'd sketched, sculpted, painted. Collette finally understood where her own passion for art came from, and it gave her a feeling of completeness. She felt blessed to have some of her mother's old paintings and sketches adorning her house. It meant the world to her.

But even better than the paintings Alison had given her, Collette had gotten to see pictures of her mother taken in the two years they'd lived together. She'd gotten to hear some wonderful stories about her mother's kind spirit. It was like having a very real piece of her to keep in her heart.

But the very best thing, the most special keepsake to come out of her experience, was a picture of her mother holding her in her arms, just days after her birth. The picture was almost identical to the painting she'd created of a mother holding her infant daughter. Coincidence? Collette didn't believe in coincidence anymore.

Some way, some how, Collette had drawn on an actual experience with her mother—feeling safe and loved in her arms—when she'd made that painting.

Every time Collette saw that picture of herself as a baby in her mother's arm, her mother smiling like Collette meant everything to her, she felt an incredible rush of emotion.

"Who practiced *imani*?" Dexter asked.

She had. Dexter had. And while it might not make sense to anyone else—except, perhaps, those who had *imani*—Collette felt her birth mother had played a direct role in her learning the truth about her life. It was as if her spirit had guided her in the right direction to find everything she needed to learn.

It had all started with that letter from her grandmother. If it hadn't been for that, she wouldn't have returned to Miami. If she hadn't returned to Miami, she wouldn't have learned about the wonderful woman who'd given birth to her.

And she never would have met up with Dexter again.

The love of her life. Her soul mate.

And now, her husband of five months. Her life was rich, full, better than she would have ever imagined, all because it had been turned upside down.

"Let us always honor our ancestors. Let us always keep the faith." Dexter sipped from the unity cup, then passed it to his right.

The reward for faith was in evidence all around the room. Felicity was with her husband, Harvey. She glowed these days. Pregnancy was definitely agreeing with her. Collette was looking forward to becoming a godmother next spring.

And while Collette wouldn't have believed it possible a year ago, she and her natural father were getting along. She believed wholeheartedly that he was sorry for what he'd done, for getting involved with her mother, but worse, for not standing beside her. She would never consider him her real father—that was Victor Jenkins—but there was room for him in her heart.

He was here tonight, as was Jabari. They'd celebrated Kwanzaa with her and Dexter all seven days. So had Alison Ball, her husband and two children. They were like her extended family.

Happiness filling her heart, Collette watched and listened as everyone drank from the unity cup and spoke of an ancestor.

Finally, the cup came to her. Before speaking, she looked up at Dexter and found him looking down at her with love.

Collette lifted the cup. "Tonight, this last day of Kwanzaa, I honor a very special person. I honor my birth mother, the wonderful woman who brought me into this world. The woman who loved me with all her heart and wished for me the very best in life. I honor Shaylee Leanne Simon."

Collette raised the cup to her lips and sipped. "May her spirit always live in my heart."

Dexter gave her a warm smile as he took the cup from her and placed it before them on the table.

"May *imani* light the way for the coming year," Dexter said. "May we live by the *nguzo saba,* and next year may we gather again, more of us, still laughing and strong. Still striving for greatness and a better life."

As Collette looked up at her husband, the man who had introduced her to this special holiday, her eyes filled with happy tears.

"*Harambee,*" Dexter said.

Everyone joined in, saying "*Harambee*" six more times.

Harambee. She and Dexter had pulled together. Together, they had found the kind of love that comes but once in a lifetime.

Two hearts. One beat. One soul.

One love.

ABOUT THE AUTHOR

Kayla Perrin spends her time between Toronto and Miami. She attended the University of Toronto and York University, where she obtained a Bachelor of Arts in English and Sociology and a Bachelor of Education, respectively. As well as being a certified teacher, Kayla works in the Toronto film industry as an actress, appearing in many television shows, commercials, and movies.

Kayla is most happy when writing. As well as novels, she has had romantic short stories published by the Sterling/MacFadden Group.

She would love to hear from her readers. E-mail her at: *kaywriter1@aol.com*. Mail letters to:

Kayla Perrin
c/o Cornerstone Literary, Inc.
4500 Wilshire Blvd.
2nd floor
Los Angeles, CA 90010

Please enclose a SASE if you would like a reply.

Coming in November from Arabesque Books . . .

__SECRET DESIRE by Gwynne Forster
1-58314-124-3   **$5.99**US/**$7.99**CAN

Victims of a harrowing robbery, widow Kate Middleton and her young son are rescued by police captain Luke Hickson. Neither of them expect, much less welcome, an instant spark of attraction. But when trouble strikes again, Kate realizes the only place she feels safe is in Luke's embrace. . . .

__SHATTERED ILLUSIONS by Candice Poarch
1-58314-122-7   **$5.99**US/**$7.99**CAN

When a hurricane damages fiercely independent Delcia Adams's island campground, she must hire Carter Matthews to help her rebuild. The more she lets him help, the more she discovers that the handsome stranger is a man of dangerous secrets . . . and irrestible fire.

__BETRAYED BY LOVE by Francine Craft
1-58314-163-4   **$5.99**US/**$7.99**CAN

All Maura Blackwell wants is money to save her grandfather's life and all her former flame Joshua Pyne wants is a child of his own. When the two strike a bargain to wed, neither of them expect an undeniable love—or the inexplicable urge to turn their make-believe marriage into the real thing.

__A FORGOTTEN LOVE by Courtni Wright
1-58314-123-5   **$5.99**US/**$7.99**CAN

As the administrator of a major ER, Dr. Joni Forest faced down personal and professional turmoil to make the unit respected. Now, the ER's former head, Dr. Don Rivers, is back, challenging her leadership—and reigniting the simmering desire between them. Now, the couple must come to terms with unresolved pain and career pressures in order to claim true love. . . .

Call toll free **1-888-345-BOOK** to order by phone or use this coupon to order by mail. *ALL BOOKS AVAILABLE NOVEMBER 1, 2000.*

Name _____

Address _____

City _____ State _____ Zip _____

Please send me the books I have checked above.

I am enclosing	$_____
Plus postage and handling*	$_____
Sales tax (in NY, TN, and DC)	$_____
Total amount enclosed	$_____

*Add $2.50 for the first book and $.50 for each additional book.

Send check or money order (no cash or CODs) to: **Arabesque Books, Dept. C.O., 850 Third Avenue, 16th Floor, New York, NY 10022**

Prices and numbers subject to change without notice. All orders subject to availability.

Visit our website at **www.arabesquebooks.com**.

Arabesque Romances
by *Roberta Gayle*

__MOONRISE   0-7860-0268-9 $4.99US/$6.50CAN
When beautiful art dealer Pascale de Ravenault and Captain Jack Devlin meet, an undeniable spark of passion is kindled . . . but the two must battle scheming revolutionaries intent on capturing a legendary masterpiece in order to save a love that has captured them both.

__SUNRISE AND SHADOWS
                 0-7860-0136-4 $4.99US/$6.50CAN
Navajo raised Roses Jordan had both grit and goodness—yet no man had ever touched her heart. Then a handsome, restless man named Tobe Hunter rode into town—searching for a way to stop running, a place to make a new life, and a woman to love . . .

__WORTH WAITING FOR
                 0-7860-0522-X $4.99US/$6.50CAN
Attorney Eliza Taylor had her life under perfect control until she was enlisted to help a friend's handsome brother, Ely, keep custody of his son. Suddenly, Eliza finds herself in the middle of a case loaded with legal curves and falling for a man who ignites her deepest hungers . . .

__BOUQUET   0-7860-0515-7 $4.99US/$6.50CAN
by Roberta Gayle, Anna Larence, & Gail McFarland
Spring is the time to celebrate the women who gave us the precious gift of life—and the irreplaceable love that sustains us. Cherish the power of a mother's love—and a mother in love—with these heartwarming tales. . . .
